Relataships & Ideas

Praise for *Ways to Live Forever*

WIN

"*Powerful, inspiring and courageous … the début of the year*"
Waterstone's

"*This is an elegant, intelligent, moving and sometimes even funny book.
Young readers (and brave parents, and teachers) will love it.*"
Guardian

"*… A Jodi Picoult for teens that pulls no punches.*"
Sue Steel, Simply Books

"*… Wonderful. Moving and funny and, yes, sad*"
Eva Ibbotson

"*Heart-wrenching… an exceedingly poignant read.*"
Bookseller

"*A deeply affecting and life-affirming read.*"
Nikki Gamble, Writeaway!

"*Sympathetic, touching and surprisingly funny … a fantastic début*"
Lovereading4kids

"*Moving, tender but also deeply humorous*"
The Bath Chronicle

"*An excellent and moving work … beautifully done*"
Irish Times

Praise from readers

"The best book I have ever read."
Sarah, age 12

"Perfect from start to finish."
Phoebe

"An excellent, inspiring book"
Mark

"This is the most AMAZING book ever, both hilarious and moving at the same time. When I got to the end I was fighting back the tears."
Nadia

"(My 11-year-old daughter) enjoyed it so much she begged me to read it ... it is an amazing book that touched me so much."
Claire

"This is a beautiful, life affirming, funny and special book. I laughed through the first half and cried through the next."
Hilary, age 31

"I will recommend this to anyone I can and will LOVE it forever."
Rebecca

"I can't remember the last time I sobbed so much and when a novel has had such a profound effect on me. I can't wait to loan (but not give!) this book to my friends."
Joy, age 39

Ways to Live Forever

SALLY NICHOLLS

MARION LLOYD BOOKS

First published in the UK in 2008 by
Marion Lloyd Books
An imprint of Scholastic Ltd
Euston House, 24 Eversholt Street
London, NW1 1DB, UK
Registered office: Westfield Road, Southam, Warwickshire, CV47 0RA
SCHOLASTIC and associated logos are trademarks and or registered trademarks of
Scholastic Inc.

Lines from *Children and Death* reprinted by permission of Routledge Publishing Inc.

Definitions of 'Death' and 'Airship' from the Concise English Dictionary (9e)
reprinted by permission of Oxford University Press.

ISBN 978 1 407105 15 4

A CIP catalogue record for this book is available from the British Library
All rights reserved

Printed in the UK by CPI Bookmarque, Croydon, CR0 4TD

www.scholastic.co.uk/zone

To Mum and Tom,
Nicola, Carolyn and Sarah.

Thank you.

CONTENTS

This is my book, started 7th January, finished 12th April. It is a collection of lists, stories, pictures, questions and facts.
It is also my story.

LIST NO. 1 FIVE FACTS ABOUT ME

1. My name is Sam.

2. I am eleven years old.

3. I collect stories and fantastic facts.

4. I have leukaemia.

5. By the time you read this, I will probably be dead.

A BOOK ABOUT US   7th January

Today was our first day back at school after the Christmas
holidays.

We have school three days a week – on Mondays,
Wednesdays and Fridays, in the living room. There are only two
pupils – me and Felix. Felix doesn't care about learning anything.

"What's the point of being ill if you have to do maths?" he said,
the first time he came to school at my house. Mrs Willis, who's our
teacher, didn't argue. She doesn't fuss if Felix doesn't do any work.
She just lets him sit there, leaning back in his chair and telling me
what's wrong with whatever I'm doing.

"That's not how you spell ammonium! We never spelt

ammonium like that at my school!"

"There's a planet called Hercules – isn't there, Mrs Willis?"

"What're you doing *that* for?"

Felix only comes to school to see me and to give his mum a break.

Nowadays, Mrs Willis thinks up ploys to interest him. You know the sort of thing; making volcanoes that really erupt, cooking Roman food, making fire with a magnifying glass.

Only my mum didn't like that one, because we accidentally burnt a hole in the dining table.

Sort of accidentally-on-purpose.

Today, though, Mrs Willis said, "How about you do some writing?" and we both groaned, because we'd been hoping for more fire, or possibly an explosion. Mrs Willis said, "Oh, come on, now. I thought you might like to write something about yourselves. I know you both like reading."

Felix looked up. He was playing with two of my Warhammer orcs, advancing them on each other and going "Grrrrah!" under his breath.

"Only 'cause there's nothing else to do in hospital," he said.

Me and Felix are both experts at being in hospital. That's where we met, last year.

I didn't see what reading had to do with writing about me and I said, "Books are just about kids saving the world or getting beaten up at school. You wouldn't write about us."

"Maybe not you," said Felix. He pressed his hand to his

forehead and flopped back in his chair. "The tragic story of Sam McQueen. A poor, frail child! Struggling bravely through *terrible* suffering and hospitals with no televisions!"

I made vomiting noises. Felix stretched his hand – the one that wasn't pressed to his forehead – out to me.

"Goodbye – goodbye – dear friends—" he said, and collapsed against his chair making choking sounds.

Mrs Willis said, "No dying at the table, Felix." But you could tell she wasn't really angry. She said, "I'd like you both to have a go now, please. Tell me something about yourself. You don't have to write a whole book by lunchtime."

So that's what we're doing. Well, I am. Felix isn't doing it properly. He's written: "My name is Felix Stranger and", and then he stopped. Mrs Willis didn't make him write any more. But I'm on page three already.

School's nearly over now, anyway. It's very quiet. Mrs Willis is pretending to do her marking and really reading *70 Things To Do With Fire* under the table. Felix is leading my orcs in a stealth attack on the pot plant. Columbus, the cat, is watching with yellow eyes.

Next door, in the kitchen, Mum is stirring the soup, which is lunch. Dad is in Middlesbrough, being a solicitor. My sister Ella is at school. Real school. Thomas Street Primary.

Any minute now – there it is! There's the doorbell. Felix's mum is here. School is over.

WHY I LIKE FACTS

I like facts. I like *knowing* things. Grown-ups never understand this. You ask them something like, "Can I have a new bike for Christmas?" and they give you a waffly answer, like, "Why don't you see how you feel nearer Christmas?" Or you might ask your doctor, "How long do I have to stay in hospital?" and he'll say something like, "Let's wait and see how you get on", which is doctor-speak for "I don't know".

I don't have to go into hospital ever again. Dr Bill promised. I have to go to clinic – that's it. If I get really sick, I can stay at home.

That's because I'm going to die.

Probably.

Going to die is the biggest waffly thing of all. No one will tell you anything. You ask them questions and they cough and change the subject.

If I grow up, I'm going to be a scientist. Not the sort that mixes chemicals together, but the sort that investigates UFOs and ghosts and things like that. I'm going to go to haunted houses and do tests and prove whether or not poltergeists and aliens and Loch Ness monsters really exist. I'm very good at finding things out. I'm going to find out the answers to all the questions that nobody answers.

All of them.

ELLA   7th January

My sister Ella went back to school today too. She and Mum had
a huge fight this morning about it. She doesn't get why I stay at
home all day and she doesn't.

"Sam doesn't go to school!" she said to Mum. "You don't go to
work!"

"I have to look after Sam," Mum said.

"You do not," said Ella. "You just do ironing and plant things
and talk to Granny."

Which is true.

My mum named me Sam, after Samson in the Bible, and my
dad named Ella after his aunt. If they'd talked to each other a bit

more while they were doing it, they might not have ended up with kids called Sam 'n' Ella, but it's too late to change that now. I think Dad thinks it's funny, anyway.

Ella's eight. She has dark hair and bright, greeny-brown eyes, like those healing stones you buy in hippie shops. No one else in my family cares what they look like. Granny goes round in trousers with patches and padded waistcoats with pockets for pencils and seed packets and train tickets. And Mum's clothes are all about a hundred years old. But Ella always fusses about what she wears. She has a big box of nail varnish and all of Mum's make-up because Mum hardly ever wears it.

"Why don't you wear it?" says Ella. "*Why?*"

Ella always asks questions. Granny said she was born asking a question and it hasn't been answered yet.

"Was I?" said Ella, when she heard this. "What was it?"

We all laughed.

"Where am I?" said Mum.

"Who're these funny-looking people?" said Granny.

"What am I *doing* here?" said Dad. "I was supposed to be a princess!"

"Who'd make *you* a princess?" I said.

It's afternoon now and I'm still writing. I bet I could write a book. Easy. I was going to do some more after Felix went, but Maureen from Mum's church came round, so I had to be visited. She only left when Mum went to fetch Ella from school. I was thinking up

"Questions Nobody Answers" at the dining table when they came back. Ella ran straight over to me.

"What are you doing?"

"School stuff," I said. I curled my arm around the page. Ella came right up behind me and peered over my shoulder.

"*Ella*. I'm busy," I said. It was the wrong thing to say. She tugged on my arm.

"Let me *see*!"

"*Mum!*" I wailed. "Ella won't let me work!"

"Sam won't let me *see*!"

Mum was on the phone. She came through with it pressed against her chest.

"Kids! Behave! Ella, leave your brother alone."

I pulled a face at Ella. She flung herself on to the sofa.

"It's not fair! You always let him win!"

Ella and Mum *always* fight. And Ella always says it's not fair. I bet that's the only reason I win, because I don't throw baby tantrums like she does.

Mum put down the phone and went over to Ella. Ella shouted, "Go away!" and ran upstairs. Mum gave this big sigh. She came over to me. I closed my pad so she wouldn't see the writing.

"Secret, is it?" she said.

"It's for school." I held my pen over the closed pad. Mum sighed. She kissed the top of my head and went upstairs after Ella.

I waited until I was quite sure she was gone, then I picked up my pen and started writing again.

QUESTIONS NOBODY ANSWERS NO. 1

How do you know that you've died?

HOW DO YOU KNOW
THAT YOU'VE DIED?   9th January

Today we had school again. I told Mrs Willis I was going to write
a book.

"It's about me," I said. "But also it's a scientific inquiry. I've
done loads." And I showed her my first "Question Nobody
Answers".

"Very commendable," she said. "How exactly are you going to
find the answers to these things?"

"I'm going to look them up on the Internet," I said.

You can find out anything on the Internet.

Mrs Willis let me and Felix look up how you know that you've died today. We had to bring Dad's laptop down from the study, because Felix has a wheelchair at the moment. When I first met him he was only in it some of the time, but he's almost always in it now. He can walk really. He just likes having people wait on him.

We started with www.ask.com and ended up with this website on near-death experiences. A near-death experience is when someone almost dies but changes their mind at the last minute and comes back. The website said this happens to five per cent of adult Americans.

"So they *say*," said Felix.

All sorts of things happened to these people, according to the website. They went down dark tunnels. They saw bright lights and angels. Sometimes they floated over their body and saw their doctors talking about them or giving them electric shocks. It was exactly the sort of science I want to do. I thought it was brilliant. Felix didn't.

"It's not real," he said. "How can everyone see angels? What about serial killers?"

Mrs Willis made us write out all of the evidence for and against, like a proper scientific study. It was yet another ploy to make Felix do something, but it worked. He wrote eight whole sentences "Against".

Near-Death Experiences – Against
by Felix Stranger

Near-death experiences aren't actual death experiences because people don't actually die. They're just people's brains going funny because they haven't had enough oxygen or are on weird drugs. If they're real, then why do different things happen to different people? And why do only good things happen? Why don't people get devils or something? Also, it's the sort of thing people make up to get attention. Like crop circles. Everyone thought they were made by spaceships, but actually it was just farmers with lawnmowers trying to be famous.

He was the cynical public. I was the groundbreaking scientist, so I did "For".

Near-Death Experiences – For by Sam McQueen

Near-death experiences have been happening since Plato, who lived thousands of years ago. We know because he wrote about them. In a near-death experience, the person actually dies. And then comes back. So obviously what happens to them is real. Also, they see real things. For example, one woman was floating on the ceiling and she heard

her doctors saying all this stuff which she found
out later that they'd actually said. Only she
couldn't have known about it because she was
dead at the time. And bad things do happen to
people sometimes. One guy had elves poking him
with pitchforks.

Mrs Willis said we clearly had very scientific minds and she was sorry she'd ever doubted us. Felix and I spent the rest of the lesson planning our perfect near-death experience. We got a bit stuck because we both wanted to go to Heaven, but only if we got the elves with pitchforks as well.

LIST NO. 2   FIVE FACTS ABOUT HOW I LOOK

1. I have hair. It all fell out last year because of the drugs I was on, but it's grown back now. It's light brown.

2. I have blue eyes.

3. I have quite a lot of bruises. It's not my fault. It's just what you get when you have leukaemia.

4. I am small for eleven and sort of pale.

5. I have a birthmark shaped like a four-leafed clover on my knee. But it doesn't grant wishes.

My mum used to work for this charity that does things with kids with learning disabilities. She stopped when I got ill the second time. Now she stays at home and takes me to clinic and looks after everyone who comes to visit. She gets Sundays off to go to church and sing in the choir. Ella goes sometimes too, but only because everyone fusses over her. I used to as well but I don't now, because I hate people fussing over me. Dad never does.

Dad is very clever. He knows a lot of things, but I could never ask him any of my questions. He doesn't talk about me being ill. I've never tried to talk to him about it, but Granny has and some of my aunties. He just says, "We're not going to talk about this," and walks out of the room.

I have a lot of aunties and uncles. Mum has one brother, but Dad has one brother and four sisters. Mum says that's why he's so quiet and likes having time to read the newspaper in peace, because he never got any space when he was a kid. I think that's rubbish, because my aunts and uncle never got any space either and they're always talking and laughing.

Dad's just quiet, like me. He's shy. When it's just our family, he's not quiet. He talks and tells jokes and stories. He knows a lot of stories. He just doesn't like it when there're loads of people in the house, like now when they keep coming to visit us. He reads his newspaper and doesn't talk, or if it's people he really doesn't like, he goes and reads in the study.

I don't think there's anything wrong with that. I wish I could go and hide sometimes too.

Granny gets angry with Dad sometimes, because she says he makes Mum do everything. But Dad does do things. He earns money. And he *does* help. Like one time when I was in hospital, Mum got home and there were four different types of soup on the doorstep. Dad and Ella heated them all up and brought them back to hospital and gave a cup to all the people waiting in casualty.

Everyone thought they were mad. But it got rid of the soup.

LIST NO. 3 THINGS THAT I WANT TO DO

1. Be a famous scientist. Find things out and write books about them.

2. Break a world record. Not an athletic one, obviously. A silly one.

3. Watch all the horror films I'm not allowed to watch. 15-certificates. Or 18s.

4. Go up down-escalators and down up-escalators.

5. See a ghost.

6. Be a teenager. Do teenage things like drink and smoke and have girlfriends.

7. Ride in an airship.

8. Go up in a spaceship and see the Earth from space.

THE OCCASIONAL WARDROBE
NIGHTCLUB   13th January

It was Mrs Willis who told me about things to do. She said we
should make a list.

"Things I want to do. Or just things I want. Preferably
achievable but not necessarily."

There are lots of things I want to do. I liked writing them down.
Mrs Willis liked it too. She wrote:

1. Go to the Grand Canyon.
2. Clean out the attic.
3. Get the use of a proper laboratory.
4. Learn how to make meringues.

5. Train the dog.

"Train the dog!" said Felix. "What sort of a wish is that?"
    "You haven't met the dog," said Mrs Willis.
    Felix's list was very short. It said:

1. Be rich and famous.
2. Nuke all doctors.
3. See Green Day in concert.

"You've already seen Green Day in concert," I pointed out. "You
went with your brother."
    Felix bent over his list again. "There," he said. "Happy?"
    It now said:

3. See Green Day in concert AGAIN.

It was a good lesson. We spent the rest of it drawing pictures of
people nuking Green Day from airships, with borders of beer-
drinking ghosts going up escalators.

After Mrs Willis had gone, Felix and I stayed at the table. I started
laying out my Warhammer army, in the hope that he might give me
a game. Felix bent over my list with his hat pulled down over his eyes.
He wears hats a lot because the drugs they gave him last year made
his hair fall out. They made mine fall out too, but it's grown back now.

Felix's hasn't. He was wearing his fedora today, which is sort of like a squashed bowler hat. It made him look like a scruffy James Bond.

"Are you going to actually do these?" he said.

"I dunno," I said. I was more interested in laying out my scenery. "Probably not. Why?"

"Well, we could. Couldn't we?" He looked across at me, daring me to argue. I sifted through my box of pieces, trying to find another archer.

"They aren't things to do really," I explained. "They're more like . . . wishes. Not real things."

Felix leaned forward. He likes an argument. "So?" he said. "Mrs Willis is going to make meringues, isn't she? So why can't we watch horror films? Mickey's got loads at home."

He shoved the list across the table towards me. I looked at it.

"We could do two of them," I said. I knelt on the seat of my chair and leaned across the table to show him. "Look. We could watch horror films and go up down-escalators. Maybe. We couldn't do the others."

"We could do a world record."

"You don't just *do* world records."

I went and fetched my *Guinness Book of Records* to show him. I love world records. I love how certain they are. The quickest anyone has ever jumped up the steps of the CN tower on a pogo stick *is* fifty-seven minutes and fifty-one seconds.* The longest

*Ashrita Furman, on 23rd July 1999. Ashrita Furman has broken over sixty world records, including the record for the person to break the most world records.

word in English with each letter in it at least twice *is* "unprosperousness". There it is, a true fact, written down in this book, and if you can beat it you just send a letter to the record people and they check it and then you go in the book as a true fact too. Plus, you get to be famous.

Felix took the book from me and started flicking through it, looking for an easy one.

"Most worms eaten in thirty seconds! Do that one!"

I remembered that record. I peered over his shoulder. "That guy ate two hundred worms. I'm not eating *two hundred* worms!"

"Two hundred and one," said Felix. I ignored him. He flicked over the pages. "Smallest nightclub in the world: 2.4 × 2.4 × 1.2 metres. That's not a proper record! How old is this book?"

"I got it for Christmas."

Felix shook his head. "Anyone can build a nightclub. What d'you need – music?"

"And strobe lights . . . and a smoke machine. . ." I read.

Felix waved his hand dismissively. "You don't need all that. Let's just put a CD player in your wardrobe."

"That's not a record!"

"Why not?"

"Lots of reasons!" I never win arguments with Felix. "Clubs are open to the public."

"So are we. We're just a bit rubbish at advertising." He grinned. "Go on – fetch a CD player. Don't you want the record?"

I pulled a face at him. But I went and got the CD player from the kitchen anyway. When I got back, Felix was in my room, peering into my wardrobe. My room used to be the garage, so it's on the ground floor. It's pretty big. It's got chunky blue furniture that all matches and lots of posters: a Spiderman one, one of the solar system, one of *Lord of the Rings* and one of a wolf that my uncle got me from Canada.

"Is there a plug?" said Felix, as I came in. He'd got my Maglite torch and was shining it into the wardrobe.

"It's got batteries." I dumped the CD player in the wardrobe and turned it on. "Don't Stop Me Now" started playing. Felix groaned. I laughed.

"No wonder we don't have any customers!"

"Who cares?" said Felix. "Look. We've got music. We've got lighting." He turned on the torch and swirled it vaguely into the wardrobe. "Hey – we've even got a moving dance floor." He spotlighted my old skateboard, propped up against the back of the wardrobe. "World record. What more do you want?"

I laughed. Felix always makes me laugh. "Look," he said, "if you still think it doesn't count, we'll start our own record. Smallest occasional wardrobe nightclub. I bet no one's broken that one."

"Only because no one would! Who'd set a record like that?"

"Who'd pogo stick up the CN building?" said Felix. He was laughing too. "Who cares if it's stupid? It's still a record, isn't it?"

"It really isn't. A record is more impressive than that!"

Felix looked up at me. You could see he was plotting something.

"Not a problem," he said.

These are the new (unofficial) records Felix and I set before Felix's mum came.

1. Sam McQueen and Felix Stranger: smallest occasional wardrobe nightclub: The Coathanger Club.
2. Felix Stranger: most cornflakes eaten in fifteen seconds: five handfuls.
3. Sam McQueen: shortest time to hop up a flight of stairs (holding on to the banister): forty-three seconds.
4. Felix Stranger: most times to recite the alphabet all the way through, without mistakes, in thirty seconds: nine.
5. Banned (Mum): shortest time to hop up a flight of stairs (not holding on to the banister).

QUESTIONS NOBODY ANSWERS NO. 2

Why does God make kids get ill?

A BLOODY BATTLE   13th January

I spent all day today writing about Felix and the lesson and the record. Sometimes, since I got ill this last time, I just get tired. All I want to do is curl up and watch films, or look at a book, or write and write and not have to think. Today was like that. Dad came home early from work, so Mum could take Ella off to buy shoes. It was nice having Dad to myself. Even if all he did was read his book. And then Mum and Ella came back.

"Home at last!" said Mum. Mum hates buying things with Ella. They always fight. She dumped her bags on the floor and looked at us. "Haven't you two moved since we left? Sam, whatever are you doing? Writing a novel?"

I closed my pad. I didn't want her to see what I *was* doing. She gets upset, Mum. I knew how upset she'd get by some of what I've written. Like the questions. Dad just ignores things like that, but Mum cries.

"It's for school."

"You're doing an awful lot of school work all of a sudden, aren't you?"

Dad looked up. "He's done nothing but write all afternoon," he said. He pushed his glasses up his nose. "If you're putting that much effort into your homework, don't you think it's time you went back to school? That poor woman's been coming out here long enough."

"I like Mrs Willis," I said quickly. I don't want to go back to school. The kids all stare and ask questions. Like: "How come you get to go home when you get tired?" Or: "How sick are you *really*?"

"Daniel. . ." Mum said, in her warning voice. Ella was staring. Dad shook his head.

"It's ridiculous. Anyone can see how much better Sam is now. It's silly to keep him cooped up here with nothing to do. . ."

"I've got lots of things to do," I said. "Dad. Don't. I'm fine."

"Daniel. . ." said Mum, again. All of the smile had gone out of her face. "Daniel, don't start all that again. *Please*. Not in front of the children."

Ella was tugging on Mum's sleeve. "Mum? Mum? What's the matter? *Mum?*"

Mum didn't answer. She was looking at Dad. Dad looked sort of guilty and determined at the same time.

"I don't think that doctor knew what he was talking about," he said. "Sam's doing great. Just look at him."

They all looked at me. Ella screamed. "Sam!"

I put my hand up to my face. It was covered in blood.

Mum shot this look at Dad, like it was his fault. Which it wasn't. She came and knelt down beside me. "All right, Sam. Lean forward. There you go. It's just a nosebleed. Daniel – *Daniel* – don't just sit there – go and get some tissues. All right, Sam."

I get nosebleeds a lot. I hate it. I hate everyone fussing. Ella being a helpful Brownie, passing tissues to Mum. Mum telling me what to do, like I don't already know. And Dad. Not moving. Just sitting there. Watching, with this odd look on his face.

I ducked my head, and pretended that some strong wind had swept right through the house and blown them all away. I stared instead at the drops of blood, still falling – drip – drip – drip – out of my cupped hands and on to the floor.

And now I'm tied to a pole. This also happens a lot.

After my nosebleed stopped, Mum phoned Annie. Annie's my special nurse, from hospital. She's crazy. She's got this pink scooter that she rides everywhere. She calls herself Dracula because she's always taking kids' blood to do tests on.

"What've you been up to, then?" she said, as she sat down next to me to take a blood sample. I took my T-shirt off so she could get at my Hickman Line. A Hickman Line is this long, skinny tube that I've got stuck in my chest. They use it to take blood and give me stuff through. It's pretty boring, but it's a pain because it's always there and you can't ever forget you're ill.

I don't know what Annie expected me to answer. I thought about everything that was happening – this book, the things Felix and I have started doing, my questions, Dad saying Dr Bill had got it wrong and maybe I was going to get better after all.

"Nothing," I said.

After Annie had gone, things stayed gloomy. What usually happens when I have nosebleeds and things is I get given platelets – I get them about once a week – but before I do they have to do tests on my blood. So while we were waiting for the results, Mum clattered about being angry and Dad skulked at the end of the table, not being sorry. Eventually, he went into the kitchen after Mum. Ella and I could hear them talking in low voices, but we couldn't tell if they were fighting or making up.

And I did need platelets. Annie brought them from the hospital just now. They're yellow and squidgy and they come in a floppy bag, like blood. You hook them on to a metal pole* and they go in through your line. They're the bits in blood that make scabs and stop it all running out when you cut yourself.

That's all you can say about platelets, really.

*It's called an IV stand. I've got my own IV stand with vampire stickers stuck all over it. They don't actually tie you to it. It just feels like it.

THE FRENCH SPY OR
THE STORY OF HOW I MET FELIX

Remember I told you I collected stories, right at the start? True ones are best. This is a true story. It's the story of how I met Felix.

It was last year, when I was in hospital for six whole weeks. I'd only been there a couple of days when I met him. It was evening and the whole children's ward had this dark, end-of-day kind of feel to it. I was lying on my bed with the door open, so I could look into the corridor. There wasn't much to see. Most people had gone home. I wasn't reading or watching television or playing on my Gameboy. I was just looking at the fuzzy reflections of the lights on the hospital floor, feeling bored and tired and sort of heavy, when this boy went past in a wheelchair.

He was a very skinny boy, a bit older than me. He was wearing tracksuit bottoms, a black T-shirt and this black beret pulled down over one ear. It made him look like a French spy, or someone in the French resistance in the Second World War.

He was acting like a spy too. He wheeled himself to the end of the corridor where the nurses' station was. Then he peered around the corner, just quickly. Then he reversed back into my corridor. Then he did the same thing again. He must have decided that the coast was clear, because he disappeared right round the corner. But he was soon back, reversing at top speed as if all the Nazis in the hospital were on to him. I sat up in bed, expecting to see someone coming after him, but no one was.

I reckoned he was putting it on, mostly, because he really didn't need to do all that forwards-and-backwardsing just to look round a corner. I leaned forward in bed, wondering what he was going to do next.

And then he turned and saw me looking.

We stared at each other through my open bedroom door. Then he swept off his beret and bowed to me, as well as he could in his wheelchair. That's when I saw he'd lost his hair, so I knew he had cancer. I kept staring at him, until I realized he was expecting me to do something. So I bowed back, very serious. Then I looked up quickly to see what he was going to do next.

He put his finger to his lips to show that I wasn't to say anything. I nodded. He nodded back, once, and rammed the beret on to his head. He gave me this sort of salute with two fingers, as if to say, "So long, comrade", or something like that. Then he turned and struck out for the nurses' station.

I sat there, waiting. I was sure I'd see him again.

He'd only been gone half a minute when he came back, reversing frantically. Only this time he came right up to my room and in through the door. He scrabbled for the door edge with his fingers, caught it, and flung it back.

The door shut with a slam.

Behind us, we heard the sound of someone's bed rattling down the corridor.

We sat there, me in my bed, he in his chair, staring at each other.

I went shy. Felix didn't. Felix isn't ever shy. I would never have barged into some strange kid's room without asking, but he wasn't bothered at all.

"Phewf," he said. And he took off his beret and wiped his forehead. Not that his forehead was really sweaty. He was just doing it for effect. Now he was so close, I could see what was written on his T-shirt. It said "GREEN DAY american idiot", and had this picture of a white hand squeezing a red heart. The picture had all these little lines down it, where it was worn away from too much washing.

"Why're you hiding?" I said.

"I'm going to the shop," said the boy. He fumbled in the cloth pocket on the side of his wheelchair and pulled something out, fingers curled around it so any stray Nazi parachutists in the corridor wouldn't be able to see what it was. It was a packet of cigarettes.

"Where did you get those from?" I said, staring.

"The machine in my uncle's pub," he said. "Only I'm out and I want some more." He put the empty packet lovingly back into the pocket. "If I can get past *them*," – he jerked his head towards the nurses' station – "then maybe I could get someone downstairs to buy me some. You know, tell them my last dying wish on earth is for a cigarette."

He grinned at me, daring me to say something.

I liked him already.

"It wouldn't work," I said. "You'd do better to tell them that you've got a very rich dying uncle looking for an heir and *his* last wish is a cigarette. People don't care about rich uncles dying of too many cigarettes, but they do kids."

The boy raised his eyebrows. "Worth a try," he said. "Are you coming?"

I hesitated. "Why're you worried about the nurses?" I said. "No one's going to care if you go to the shop, are they?"

The boy tapped his nose mysteriously. "It's to get them off our scent," he said. "Like, say they smell smoke in my room. If I haven't left the floor, it can't have been me, can it? How would I get cigarettes? So it must've been a visitor or someone. See?"

I did. Kind of. Actually, I thought they'd be way more suspicious if they caught him trying to sneak past them. But I knew that wasn't the point.

It was a game. The nurses were the enemy. We were the resistance army.

It wasn't hard getting past the nurses' station. There was only one nurse there anyway, so I told her that the little kid in the room next to mine was making a racket. Which was true.

As soon as she was gone, Felix cried, "Go! Go!" and we were off – full-speed down the corridor to freedom.

We had great fun trying to get people to buy Felix cigarettes. Felix started with the uncle story, but no one believed him. And if he said he was dying, they just looked shocked and hurried away. So we had to think of other things.

I told a nice-looking woman with two little kids that my sister was having an operation and the surgeon needed cigarettes to stop his hands shaking. She just laughed and told me to find another surgeon.

Felix told an old man he was getting withdrawal symptoms from cigarettes, which was very dangerous in his weakened condition. That was a mistake. The old man started telling him all about what happened to him when *he* quit smoking. Felix kept nodding like he was really interested and the man kept saying, "Don't believe what they tell you. Ninety-five, I am. Ninety-five!"

Felix and I kept looking at each other and trying not to laugh.

I told a weedy-looking man with a beard that I was doing a school project on how many people on a cancer ward would take a cigarette. He told me to use a questionnaire instead.

In the end, Felix told this teenage girl that a kid on the children's ward was going to beat us up if we didn't buy him some cigarettes. I don't think she believed him, but she bought the cigarettes anyway.

And after that, Felix and I were friends.

WHY DOES GOD MAKE
KIDS GET ILL?   16th January

Today, school was at Felix's house, so Mum could go and see one
of her friends for the day. Felix lives on the other side of
Middlesbrough in this little terrace house, which always smells of
dog. They've got this fat, flat dog called Maisy. She's the colour of
a doormat and she's got this really dopey, surprised expression.
Felix always has dog hairs on his bed, but he doesn't care.

Mrs Willis let us play Top Trumps instead of school. She said if
anybody asked, it was maths.

We also did my new question.

As a list.

Mrs Willis started it. "Right," she said, when I showed her my question. "Why does God make kids get ill? What do you think? How many solutions can you come up with before twelve?"

Felix said, "He doesn't exist. It's obvious. That's why."

"That's not a reason!" I said.

"Of course it is," said Felix. "He might not. Go on. Write it down."

I wrote it down.

1. He doesn't exist.

"Number two—" I began, but Felix beat me to it.

"Number two," he said, leaning forward. "Number two – he does exist but he's secretly evil. He likes torturing little kids for fun."

"I'm not putting that!" I said.

"Why not?" said Felix. "It might be true. And don't tell me you've never thought it."

I didn't answer.

"There you go," said Felix. "Number two – go on— "

2. God is really evil.

"We're only having nice ones now," I said firmly.

"There aren't any nice ones," said Felix. "How can there be? Someone gives kids cancer, they don't do it to be *nice.*" He glared at me, like it was my fault.

I thought for a moment, then wrote:

3. God is like a big doctor. He makes people ill so's to make them better, the same way doctors give people chemotherapy to make them better. It doesn't matter to God if you die, because you just go to heaven, which is where he lives anyway.

"That's rubbish!" said Felix, reading over my shoulder.

"It's what my mum thinks," I said defensively.

"How does having cancer make you *better*?"

"Well –" I hesitated. "It teaches you stuff."

"Like?"

"Well . . . like. . ." I floundered. "Like, what's important in life. I dunno. You get all excited about being able to ride your bike. And . . . and you realize how important your family are. Stuff like that."

"That," said Felix, "is the biggest load of crap I ever heard. God gives you cancer to teach you how good *riding a bike* is? You can't put that there!"

"It's there now," I said. I looked up. "Go on," I said. "You think of another one."

"There is no reason," said Felix. "It just happens."

4. There is no reason.

"*5.,*" I said. "*There is a reason, but we're too stupid to understand it.*" I looked pointedly at Felix. He laughed.

"Not very educational, your book, is it?" he said. But he was enjoying himself. You could tell. "It's punishment for being bad," he said.

"It is not!" I said.

"Why not?" Felix leaned forward. "That's what Buddhists say. They think everything that happens in this life is karma for what you did in all your other ones. So maybe we were both bank robbers or something in another life and this is payback. You can't not put it in! What if you publish your book? You'll get all these Buddhist kids reading it, all peeved 'cause they know why you're ill and it's not there! That's discrimination!"

"Buddhists aren't anything to do with God," I said. "Buddhists don't believe in God. They believe in . . . in Buddha."

"Atheists don't believe in God either," said Felix. "And their reason is first of all."

I hesitated. I didn't think we were ill because we'd done something wrong, any more than I thought Hitler was leader of Germany as a reward for doing something good. But he was right. I couldn't not put it in.

6. We did something awful in a past life and this is punishment.

"There!" said Felix with satisfaction. "What next?"

I didn't say anything. I was thinking about what Felix had said, about the Buddhist kids. What if I do write a whole book? If I do, I don't want kids to read it and go around thinking it's their fault they're ill, because they'd done something wrong.

"7," I said. *"We're perfect already. We don't need to learn anything else. Being ill is a present. Like . . . like a Get-Into-Heaven-Free Card."*

"A Get-Into-Heaven-Free Card!" said Felix.

"It's not as stupid as it sounds," I told him. "In the olden days, when kids used to die all the time, they used to think that. 'He was too good for this earth.' That's what they used to say. Or, 'God loved him so much, he wanted him in Heaven.'"

"That's rubbish," said Felix. "I'm not perfect." He shook his head. "Anyone reads your book, they're going to think you're insane," he said. "First you tell them it's a punishment, then you say it's a present for being good!"

"It's just a list!" I said. "They aren't all true at the same time!"

Felix pulled a face.

"Idiot," I said.

LIST NO. 4 FAVOURITE THINGS

1. Favourite animal: wolves. True fact: wolves have their taste buds in their stomach not their mouth. That's why they wolf down their food.

2. Favourite film: Lord of the Rings. I read the whole book too, when I was ill last year. True fact: Mordor is based on Birmingham.

3. Favourite place: High Strawberry, the holiday cottage we used to stay in in the Lake District. It was right on the shore of Lake Windermere and it had a boat.

4. Favourite game: Warhammer

5. Favourite joke: Why did the hedgehog cross the road? To show his girlfriend he had guts.

6. Favourite method of transport: airships. True fact: the reason the Empire State Building

has a spike on top is so you can tie your
airship up to it.

7. Favourite memory: white-water rafting in
Germany on holiday, before I got ill again.

TOO DISTURBING FOR
HOME VIEWING   17th January

After class, I had pizza with Felix and his mum. Afterwards, I said to Felix, "Shall we go to your room?" He has loads more music than me and some good games as well.

Felix shook his head. He put his hand up to his mouth and said in a French resistance sort of whisper, "Let's go to Mickey's room . . . less chance of being interrupted. . ."

"Why—"

"Shh!"

You always know when Felix is planning something. He has this secretive air, like he knows something and you don't. He had it now. He wouldn't tell me anything until we got up to Mickey's room, which took ages because he's not very good at climbing stairs. Mickey is Felix's brother. He works on an oil rig, one month on and one month off.

When we *finally* got up to his room, Felix said, "Listen. You know you wanted to see horror films. . ."

"Yes," I said cautiously.

"Well, look!"

He was sitting on Mickey's bed. He pulled something out from behind the pillow and flourished it at me.

"*The Exorcist!*"

I grabbed it off him. We read the back of the box eagerly.

"'Inspired by real events . . .'"

"'*The Exorcist* has, until now, been considered too disturbing for home viewing . . . one of the most shocking and gripping movies ever made.'"

"Have you seen it?"

Felix shook his head. "I only found it yesterday. It's supposed to be the worst film ever though. People used to faint in cinemas. . . There's this one bit where the girl's head spins all the way around. . ."

"What's so scary about that?" I said.

"I don't know," Felix admitted. "But it's an 18, so it must be pretty bad. And if you're going to watch a horror film, this is the one to watch."

We shut Mickey's door and turned on his DVD.

It was dead boring. We kept expecting monsters or demons or

something to appear, but nothing did. There was a whole bit that looked like something out of *Indiana Jones*, except that nothing happened apart from this old guy digging up coins. We both thought they were probably evil, possessed demonic coins, but they weren't.

Then it got confusing. There was a long bit with this kid and her mum, but it kept getting mixed up with some priest who didn't seem to have anything to do with anything. All he did was drink whisky and visit his mother. The most exciting thing that happened was the girl playing with a Ouija board, but even that wasn't particularly scary.

Nothing *too* bad happened to the girl after she'd done the Ouija board, but you could kind of tell something was going to. There was a funny scene where she wet herself at a party. And then there was a great long bit in a hospital, which neither of us liked much, so Felix tried to fast-forward and find the head-going-round-backwards scene.

I don't know if what he found was the bit that made people faint, but it was horrible. There was a room with curtains flapping and books flying around and the kid stabbing herself with a cross and there was blood everywhere and she was saying all this horrible stuff in a voice that didn't sound like hers and her face had gone all weird and I was just thinking how awful it would be if that was *you* and something was making *you* do that and—

And then Felix's mum walked into the room.

Felix's mum wouldn't let us watch the rest. Felix made a big fuss, going on about how if we didn't know how it ended we'd be haunted by the kid with the blood for ever after, but she wouldn't listen.

"She gets cured," she said. "End of story. Now go and blow up some aliens or something."

Secretly, I was glad we didn't watch any more. There was something about the idea of something living in your body and making you do creepy stuff that I didn't like. We spent the rest of the afternoon playing on Felix's computer. But after that I couldn't stop wondering about whatever it was that had happened to that kid. "Inspired by real events", it said on the box. What did that mean? What if it was really true? *Could* something like that happen to you?

I worried about it all afternoon and most of the evening, until Granny said would I stop moping for goodness' sake, because it was driving her crazy. She'd come back from taking Ella to Brownies and stayed to talk to Mum. Only Mum'd gone to answer the phone.

"Have you and that boy been up to something again?" she said.

"No," I said*, and then, "Do you believe in demons?"

"Demons?" said Granny. "You mean with horns and pitchforks?"

"No," I said. "Like . . . evil spirits. That possess people."

---

*Which was true. Felix's mum stopped us.

"No," said Granny firmly. "Absolute rubbish."

"But you believe in ghosts and things," I said.

"There's no point in inventing devils to be scared of," said Granny, very sternly. "We've enough real things to worry about without making up more for ourselves."

"Right," I said. "And I wasn't scared. I only wondered."

It wasn't really a very comforting thing for Granny to say, when you think about it. But after that I wasn't worried any more.

MY LIFE IN HOSPITALS

It's Tuesday today. We don't have school on Tuesdays, because I have clinic. Felix doesn't go to my clinic, because he doesn't have leukaemia like me. He goes to a different one, on Thursday. I know I ought to say what clinic was like, but I'm not going to. It's not very exciting. They weigh you and measure you and do blood tests and talk to you and give you some drugs there and some drugs to take home. That's it, really.

I can see why Dad thinks I'm getting better, but it's only because I'm on different drugs now. See, when you get leukaemia they give you chemotherapy, which is poison. It's not supposed to kill you, it's supposed to kill the cancer, but you get sick too. Your hair falls out and your skin burns and all sorts of stuff. So of course I'm better now I'm not having it any more.

I've had it twice. Dad wanted me to have it again, but they said no.

Leukaemia always comes back. They think they've cured it, then it comes back. Not to everyone. True fact: eighty-five per cent of people get properly cured forever. That's eight-and-a-half out of every ten people. Eighty-five out of every hundred. Eight hundred and fifty out of every thousand.

That's most people.

But it always comes back to me.

Leukaemia is a type of cancer. What happens is, your body makes too many white blood cells.* White blood cells are like your own personal resistance army. They fight infections and stuff. But when you get leukaemia they take over and the other blood cells get scrunched up and can't do all the things they're supposed to do. So you get ill. Like, you might get very pale or get loads of bruises or nosebleeds that won't stop or you feel tired all the time.

I've had it three times, including now. The first time was when I was six. I was in hospital having chemotherapy for a month and I had to take pills for ages afterwards. But they thought they'd cured it, for sure.

*In my type, acute lymphoblastic leukaemia, my body makes too many lymphoblasts, which are baby white blood cells. But the result is the same.

It came back again when I was ten. That's when I met Felix. They gave me the chemotherapy drugs then as well and my hair fell out again and everything. And they thought they'd cured it then too. Well, kind of.

"Let's wait and see," they said. Or, "Fingers crossed." And Mum looked scared and Dad went quiet.

Mum and Dad are good at being scared and quiet. And this time they were right. It did come back again. After only two and a half months.

CAPTAIN CASSIDY   21st January

When Dad came home from work last night, he didn't read his newspaper like usual. He came and watched me working. I was looking through my Warhammer magazine, trying to find pictures to stick in my book.

"Is this the great school project again?" he said. A funny smile was twitching round his lips. I think he could see it was more than just a project.

I hesitated. Then, even though I knew it was probably stupid, I said it. "I'm writing a book."

"A book!" Dad raised his eyebrows. "I tried to write a book when I was your age. *Captain Cassidy and the Castle of Doom* it was called."

"What happened?" I said. Dad laughed.

"I don't know," he said. "I never got beyond chapter one."

"My book's about me," I said.

Dad stopped laughing. "About you?"

"About . . . being ill. And everything."

"Ah." Dad was quiet. I waited for him to say something else but he didn't. I bent my head over the magazine. The silence stretched and stretched and then, suddenly, I heard his chair scrape. I looked up quickly, but he'd gone.

I thought that was it, but I was wrong. Today, when he came home from work, he had a present for me. It was a ring binder with Spiderman on it, a new tube of Pritt Stick and some sugar paper.

"For your book," he said.

"Thanks," I said. "That's . . . thanks."

"That's all right," he said. He sat down in his chair and opened his paper. Then he lowered it again. "Just one thing," he said. "You're not writing a weepy book full of poems and pictures of rainbows, are you?"

"No," I said. I wasn't sure what kind of book he was talking about, but it didn't sound like mine. "It's not that sort of book," I said.

"That's all right, then," said Dad, opening his paper again.

DR BILL

When my leukaemia came back for the third time, we had to go and talk about it with Dr Bill. He's a paediatric oncologist, which is a cancer doctor for kids. He wears this red headscarf with white dots, like a pirate. He does it so's the kids with no hair don't feel so bad. His real name is Dr William Bottomley, but no one ever calls him that.

"How can I work with you lot with a name like Dr Bottomley?" he says, and everyone laughs. So he's Dr Bill.

Dad wanted me to have more treatment, but Dr Bill said he didn't think it would work because I wasn't strong enough after the last lot. He said it was too dangerous.

"Can't we try it anyway?" said Dad and Dr Bill pursed up his lips.

"We could," he said. "But it would mean spending a lot of time in hospital again. And as it hasn't been successful this time. . ."

I knew what he meant. I'd have to have all those chemicals and get sick again but this time they already knew it wouldn't work.

"I don't want to," I said. "It's poison."

"It's poison that works," said Dad.

But Dr Bill shook his head.

"Not this time."

So what I get now are different drugs. It's still chemotherapy, but it's not the sort that makes you get sick or your hair fall out. It doesn't try and cure you, it just stops you getting worse. Although I still get tired a lot and have nosebleeds and stuff like that.

They could work for a long time, these new drugs, Dr Bill says. People can live for a whole year or more. I've had four months already.

A year's a long time.

Anything can happen in a year.

ESCALATORS

22nd January

Going up down-escalators or down up-escalators is a stupid last wish.

I've wanted to do it for ages, though. Ever since I read this book where this dog did. I think it was a magic dog. I can't remember. It wasn't like he didn't know which escalator was which; he just did it to be daring. Because it was cool. So then I wanted to too. Does that make sense?

It sounds like an easy wish to do, but actually it isn't. I'm not allowed into town by myself. And how would I explain it to Mum? "Oh, is this the down-escalator? I thought it was the up. I wondered why it was taking so long to get to the top."

She'd think I was crazy.

Maybe I am. But I still want to do it.

I've been into town with Mum a couple of times since I wrote my list and each time I've thought I'll do it and then chickened out. I had half an idea of getting Mickey to take me and Felix next time he's home. But today Mum took me to the dentist* and afterwards we had lunch in the shopping centre. It was pretty much empty. And there were two escalators.

One up.

And one down.

All the time we were eating, I couldn't stop thinking about them. Felix is right. There's no point having wishes if you don't at least *try* to do them. The possible ones anyway. Going up down-escalators . . . it's not exactly hard, is it? Doing a world record is hard. And we did that.

I looked at Mum. She was fussing, as usual.

"Sam. *Sam.* Are you all right? You haven't finished your sandwich." She looked at me closely. "You aren't too tired, are you?"

"I'm not tired at all," I said. I stood up. "I'm going to the toilet."

I went out of the café and straight to the escalators. I wanted to go up the down one, I decided. I went right down to the bottom and stood there, looking up. They went from the top floor of the shopping centre into a round, open bit with a baker and a charity shop and a couple of other little shops. There weren't

*I go to a special one because chemotherapy does funny things to teeth.

many people, but there were a few.

All the way from the café, I'd been getting nervouser and nervouser. My heart swelled until it seemed to sit just under my throat. I wish I was as strong as I was before I got ill. What if I couldn't do it? What sort of idiot would I look like then? Or what if people started yelling at me for messing around with shopping centre property? Or what if there were security guards lurking somewhere?

I went and stared into the window of the charity shop. "This is stupid," I thought. "It's an easy one! You can't not do it." I went back. There was no one on the down-escalator. Before I could think any more about it, I put my hand on the rail and stepped forward.

I'd been worried about going up the steps, but I'd forgotten about the bit at the bottom where the floor moves forward. As soon as I stepped on to it, I could feel myself being pulled backwards. I didn't have time to worry though. I ploughed forward and suddenly, there I was, going up.

It wasn't as hard as I'd thought it would be. It was weird, because I was practically running up the stairs, so I felt like I ought to be going up and up and up, only of course I wasn't, because the stairs were going down. But overall, I *did* go up. Slowly. I started gasping for breath, but I didn't dare stop. And I couldn't look up, in case I fell over. Still, now I could see the flat bit at the top coming closer. Suddenly I didn't know what to do. My feet were so used to climbing, I wasn't sure they could do forward. But

I couldn't stop now, right at the top.

I took as big a step forward as I could manage and fell over. I was all right though. My hands and one knee were on the flat, not-moving ground. I pulled myself forward and stumbled to my feet, scraped and giddy, but triumphant. I did it! And no one stopped me!

There was an old lady at the top, waiting to go down.

"It's quicker if you use the other ones, dear," she said.

"I know," I said. I glanced at her. She was smiling.

"Some sort of dare, was it?" she said.

"Something like that," I said, smiling back.

QUESTIONS NOBODY ANSWERS NO. 3

What would happen if someone wasn't really
dead and people thought they were?
Would they get buried alive?

DEATH SCENE   24th January

"How're you going to die?" said Felix.

I looked at him. It was after school. He was waiting for his mum to come. I was painting one of the new dwarfs that one of Mum's friends had bought me. He was supposed to be helping, but he'd got bored and was playing with the cat instead.

"You know," I said.

He pulled a face. "In your book, I mean," he said. Mrs Willis had brought a Van de Graaff generator to class and we'd been playing with static electricity. He was still buzzing. "You can't just end it. People will wonder what happened. You'll have to have your mum sitting by your bed with a dictaphone. 'How do you feel now, Sam?' 'I see a light … I'm moving towards the light … There's all these dodgy blokes with wings and haloes flapping around. . .'"

"Shut up," I said. Felix never usually talks like this. I wasn't sure I liked it. I preferred the Felix who carried on as if everything was normal, apart from little things like being in a wheelchair or not going to school. He didn't pay any attention to me, though.

"You could write it in advance," he said. "'My death was very sad. Everyone cried. I gave a long speech about how much I was going to miss everything and how I would look down on everyone from my cloud. Everyone said how wonderful I was, and. . .'"

I threw an orc at him. He reversed out of range, laughing. Columbus meowed.

"I know!" he said. "You could ask Dr Bill if you could watch someone else dying, as research, and then pretend it was you. You could put them in your acknowledgements—"

"My what?"

"The bit where you thank everyone for helping you. You know, 'I thank Mrs Willis for giving me the idea in the first place and Felix Stranger for all the ideas I shamelessly stole off him. And Johnny Jones, or whoever, for letting me take notes when he popped it.'"

"You're mad!" I said. "Would you let some kid take notes when you died?"

Felix was wearing his fedora again. He pulled it right down so it covered his eyes. "I wouldn't care," he said. "I'm not having anyone there."

"Much you could do about it," I said. "You'd have your mum, anyway."

Felix shook his head. The hat was still down over his eyes. "You can come and take notes if you want," he said. "But I'm not having my mum. She'd hate it."

He sounded so certain that I didn't know what to say.

"I wouldn't write a death scene anyway," I said uncomfortably. "People would know." I'd been thinking about this, while he was talking. "The rest of the book is all true, that's the whole point. But people would know I couldn't write the last bit, so they'd know I was making it up."

"So?" said Felix. He pushed back his hat and reappeared. He was laughing. "Hey!" he said. "Hey, I know! What you want to do, right, is make a set of tick boxes or something, for your mum and dad to fill in. You know, like all your daft lists:

1. *Sam's death was:*
   a. Peaceful
   b. Horrible and agonizingly painful.
   c. Kind of in the middle.
   d. We don't know – we were at the chip shop.
   e. Other, please specify.

And then they could fill them in afterwards."

"That's nuts!" I said, but I was laughing at the thought of Mum and Dad filling in Felix's survey.

"It's a stroke of genius," said Felix. "It'll be the most scientific death scene in history. And then when you publish your book, I'll get all the royalties, because at this rate I'll have written most of it, and I'll go on a Caribbean cruise on the profits." He rummaged down the side of his chair for a biro. "Come on, Charles Dickens. Write this down. Number two. . ."

THE STORY OF GRANDFATHER'S FOOTSTEPS

This is another true story. At least, Granny says it's true and she doesn't lie. Hardly ever.

Granny and Grandad met during the war. He was a conscientious objector, which means he refused to join the army and kill people. He went to work on a farm instead. Granny was fourteen and she was living on the farm because of the bombs and that's how they met. I don't remember him, but I've seen pictures. Granny says he looked just like Mum, apart from the grey beard and the pipe.

He died very suddenly of a heart attack, just after Ella was born. He got up in the morning feeling fine and by the evening he was dead.

Everyone was very shocked. All the next day, Granny says, there were people in the house; Mum and Dad and us and Uncle Douglas and neighbours and everybody, fussing about making cups of tea and talking. It was only at night that they left her alone, just her all alone in the big bed where she and Grandad had slept together every night, nearly, since she was sixteen.

She didn't think she was going to fall asleep, but she must have done because she had a dream. Except she isn't sure that it *was* a dream because it felt so real. She says Grandad came into the room and sat on the edge of the bed and talked to her. He said he was very sorry and he didn't want to leave, but he had to go, and she wasn't to be frightened or feel sad or anything because he was all right. She says she cried and asked him to stay, but he just kept saying he had to go, and in the end he went.

Granny was still sad, of course. And she didn't like living on her own. But she says that whenever she felt unhappiest, she used to be able to smell Grandad's pipe smoke, as if he was still there, keeping an eye upon her.

"Did you ever see him?" I asked once.

"No," she said. "But once, when you two were staying, Ella turned to me – I can see her now, clear as day – and said, 'Who's that man with the beard?' She could only have been two or three."

"And was anybody there?" I asked.

"No," said Granny. "Just the smell of your grandad's pipe, that's all."

So Ella has seen a ghost. Except she can't remember it. And Mum has heard a ghost too. Because when I was ill for the second time, when everyone was so worried about me, Granny used to hear footsteps going down her corridor. At first she thought it was burglars, but when she went to look there was no one there. So she thought maybe she was imagining it, but then Mum stayed over one night and she could hear them too. So now Granny thinks it was Grandad, letting her know he was there when she was frightened about me.

Scientists would say none of this proves ghosts exist. It's *circumstantial evidence*, which means evidence that makes it more likely that something is true, but doesn't prove it. Granny's story is just like that. I mean, Ella was only two. The man with the beard could have been a picture, or a funny mark on the wallpaper. And the pipe smoke could have been Granny imagining things or smelling smoke from someone in the street. And maybe the footsteps were just creaky floorboards. But when you put them all together, you start to think maybe ghosts *do* exist.

I asked Granny if Grandad's footsteps had come back when I got ill this time, but she said she hadn't heard from him in a long time.

"He probably thinks I'm old enough to cope now," she said. "Or maybe he's moved on. I doubt he wants to spend his afterlife babysitting for an old stick like me."

So I don't know what I believe. I wouldn't want to spend my afterlife as a ghost either. But it made me think. And what I think is, if I were Grandad, I'd want to visit too.

ME AND MARIAN

We had class again today. I showed Mrs Willis my story, "Grandfather's Footsteps", and she told us ghost stories. There was one about two ladies who got lost in Versailles Palace garden, which was where the old French royalty used to live before the revolutionaries chopped their heads off. These two ladies said they went back in time to how it looked when Queen Marie Antoinette lived there. There were all these people in old-fashioned clothes speaking French. Felix said they'd probably got lost in some school's dress-as-a-French-queen day but Mrs Willis said no, the garden was different and everything.

I said they should've told Marie Antoinette the revolutionaries were going to chop her head off. If they'd only persuaded her to hide in a bush or something they'd have changed the whole course of history forever.

"Why bother?" said Mrs Willis. "Who needs the monarchy? Chop all their heads off, that's what I say."

Mrs Willis is a secret revolutionary.

After she'd gone, Felix said, "I think we need to do another one off your list, don't you? How about seeing a ghost?"

"How?" I said. I'd already decided this one was "probably-impossible". (Not like "Ride in an airship", for example, which is "possible-but-very-very-difficult".) "What do you want to do? Stand in a haunted house and look hopeful?"

Kids in books never have any trouble finding haunted houses, but there isn't one round here.

Felix tapped his nose and looked mysterious.

"Leave it to me," he said. "But let's go to your room. We don't want your mum to see."

Felix wouldn't say anything until we were in my room with the door shut. Then he put on this hushed voice and said, "Have you ever done a Ouija board?"

I haven't. My mum hates Ouija boards. She says you shouldn't meddle with stuff you don't understand. I told Felix and he said, "She goes to church, doesn't she? What's that if not meddling with things you don't understand?"

I hesitated. I couldn't help remembering *The Exorcist*, even though I knew it probably wasn't a very scientific film. Felix said, "Oh, come on! You want to meet a ghost, don't you? How else are we going to get one to come?"

So we did it.

Felix knew exactly what to do. He opened my writing pad and drew the Ouija board in red and black felt tip. He put all the letters of the alphabet in a big circle with the numbers up to nine in a small circle in the middle and YES and NO in two corners.

"There!" He looked round my room. "Now, it has to be properly dark and ghostly, like a séance."

We went into the kitchen. Felix stood guard (not that he needed to – Mum was upstairs, on the phone). I found a whole pack of night lights, the kitchen matches and the big torch.

"They have this sort of veil," said Felix.

"Net curtains!"

I was kneeling on the sideboard taking the net curtains down when Ella came in. She stared at us.

"What're you doing?"

"Making a Wendy house," said Felix. "Want to play?"

Ella's not stupid. "You are not."

"We're doing research," I said. "For my book."

Ella screwed up her face. She wasn't sure if we were having her on or not, but she did know whatever we were doing, we probably weren't supposed to be.

"We're going to call up a ghost," said Felix. "A great big one drippling with blood. You want to see?"

If he thought she was going to be scared, he was wrong.

"Yes! Let me come!"

"I dunno. . ." He grinned at me. Ella launched herself on him.

"Let me! I'll tell Mum!"

Felix loves an audience. He made her go and put on her bridesmaid's dress, because, he said, they always have girls in white at séances. While she was gone, we put all the candles out on saucers around the room and drew the curtains.

It was only four o'clock, so it wasn't really dark. Ella and I sat on the bed with my pad between us. Felix pushed his chair up against the bed and draped the net curtain over our heads, so it covered us completely. It was like being in a tent; dim and dappled and a little bit spooky. Felix switched on the torch and shone it under his chin, sending dark shadows leaping up his cheeks.

"*Welcome* to the Pit of Oblivion," he said, in this deep, mock-scary voice.

The idea of a Ouija board is that you put a penny or a glass in the middle of the bit of paper. Then you each put a finger on the penny or glass and any spirits hanging about make it move.

"Why do you need your fingers if the spirits move it?" I said.

"You just do," said Felix. "Otherwise it doesn't work."

None of us had a penny and we didn't want to leave our tent to get a glass, so we used a jelly baby instead. We all put our fingers on it and Felix said:

"OK. Is anyone there?"

For a moment, nothing happened. Then the jelly baby moved.

YES

Ella squealed.

"You did that!" I said.

"I did not!" said Felix. Then, before I could argue, "What is your name?"

"M-A-R-I-A-N," I read, as the jelly baby moved across the board. "Marian!"

"Marian who?"

"T-W-A-N-E-T. Pack it in!" I said. "Marie Antoinette's not spelt like that."

"Who is it?" demanded Ella. "Who is it? Sam?"

"It must be a mischievous spirit," said Felix, dead serious. "Or maybe she can't spell. Are you the Queen of France?"

YES

"Is that you moving it?" said Ella uncertainly. "How's it moving?"

"It's the power of the undead," Felix told her. "You can ask a question if you want."

"I don't want to," said Ella immediately. She looked at me. So did Felix.

"Why do I have to think of something?"

"You're the one with all the questions."

"Not for dead people!"

"She could do your whole project for you," Felix said.

I sighed. "All right. What's it like, being undead?"

"B-O-R-I-N-G." Now Ella was reading out the letters. "What do you do all day?" she added, greatly daring.

"D-R-I-N-K G-I-N."

"Felix!"

"What? It's not me!"

"A-N-D E-A-T C-A-K-E! She says she eats cake!"

"Stop messing with it!"

"I am *not* messing with it!" said Felix. "Look, let's ask her about us. Is Sam ever going to finish his book?"

I decided it was my turn to move it.

"D-E-F-I-"

Felix (or the spirit of Marian Twanet) fought towards the NO. I fought back.

And won.

YES

"How does she know that?" Ella stared, round-eyed.

"She knows everything," I said, triumphant.

TRUE FACTS ABOUT COFFINS

In the eighteenth and nineteenth centuries, people were very worried about being accidentally buried alive. To solve this problem, scientists invented safety coffins, which let anyone who'd been buried by mistake tell the outside world and get rescued.

In 1822, Dr Adolf Gutsmuth designed a coffin with an air and feeding tube. To prove it worked, he had himself buried in it. He ate a meal of soup, beer and sausages through the tube, before being dug up by his assistant.

Dr Johann Gottfried Taberger designed a coffin with a bell which could be rung using ropes and a long tube. Ropes were tied to the buried person's hands, feet and head. The tube had a mesh to stop insects flying down it and a little roof to stop the person in the coffin getting rained on.

Franz Vester designed a large square pipe which could be placed over a coffin. Inside it was a ladder, a bell and a cord. If the person in the coffin turned out to be alive and woke up, he could climb up the ladder and escape. If he wasn't well enough to move, he could ring the bell using the cord. If he turned out to be dead after all, the pipe was pulled back up and reused.

Nowadays scientists have got stethoscopes and electrocardiograms and things, so it's pretty easy to tell if somebody's dead or not. People still make safety coffins, though. In 1995, Fabrizio Caselli built a modern, high-tech coffin. To make absolutely sure that no one could be buried alive in it, it had an emergency alarm, a torch, an oxygen tank, a two-way microphone and speaker, a heartbeat sensor and a heart stimulator.

Today, three of my aunts came to visit. We get visited a lot now. Dad got to hide in his study and Ella got to go play with my cousin Kiara, but I had to sit and look polite. This is because they'd supposedly come a long way to see me. Only they *hadn't* come to see me. If they had, we'd have done something fun. We'd have tried out the remote-control plane Auntie Sarah gave me.* Or played with the computer game from Auntie Carolyn. Instead, I had to sit and listen to them yakking on and on and drinking tea.

*Auntie Sarah also gave Ella a whole lot of Sylvanian families stuff, which is good, because otherwise she moans about not getting anything. You get lots of free stuff if you're sick, but it doesn't work if you're just someone sick's sister.

It wasn't a very exciting visit.

They said, "How *are* you?" to Mum,

and she said, "Oh, you know. Doing the best we can."

And they said, "And how are *you*?" to me,

and I said, "Fine."

And then they spent three hours talking about my cousin Pete's part in some play and how much better my Auntie Sarah's eczema has been since they started buying organic vegetables.

After they'd gone, Dad came down from his study and found Mum staring at the salad drawer from the fridge.

"It's a tomato," he said to Mum. She didn't answer. "Not one of my sisters."

"Do you think we should start buying organic food?" said Mum.

"What?" said Dad.

"Organic food. It might be more healthy. For Sam. And all of us."

"I don't think it would make the slightest bit of difference," said Dad. He took the tomato out of Mum's hand and put it on the table. "Why is the window open?"

"I opened it," said Mum.

"But it's freezing!" said Dad.

Mum didn't say anything. She went back to staring at the tomato.

"Rachel?" said Dad.

"Sarah always leaves her windows open!" Mum burst out. "And nothing ever happens to her children!"

Dad stared at her. Then he came up to her and put his arms around her.

"Hey," he said, very gently.

Mum didn't say anything.

"This isn't because of anything you did."

Mum rubbed her head against his shoulder. "I know," she said in a whisper. Dad squeezed her arm.

"That's right," he said. Then he went and closed the window, very firmly.

WHY I WANT AN AIRSHIP

I want an airship. They're the best. They're kind of big hot air balloons, but shaped like a 0 lying on its side. And they've got a motor and you can steer them, so you can go wherever you want.

You can build your own mini airship in your garage. People have. I think that'd be amazing – it'd be like having your own plane, but better. You could fly it everywhere and when you got where you were going, you wouldn't need a helipad or a runway – you'd just tie up to a mountain or something and climb down the rope. And when you were done, you'd climb back up and fly on. You could wave at all the people stuck in traffic jams and laugh at them. If you saw someone you didn't like – like Craig Todd from school or my old teacher, Mr Cryfield – you could spit on them – splat! – or drop tomatoes on their head and they couldn't do anything about it.

You could go anywhere on it. Not just boring places like to the shops, but to Africa or America or anywhere. You wouldn't have to worry about tickets or passports or hanging around in airports, you'd just set off. Airships can cross seas, easy. You could tie up to the Statue of Liberty or the Leaning Tower of Pizza. And if anyone tried to stop you – "*Hasta la vista*, suckers!" – you'd just cast off and fly away.

You could go anywhere – anywhere. And no one would be able to stop you.

BE A TEENAGER

I went round to Felix's again yesterday, for the afternoon. Felix answered the door.

"Hello!" he said. He nodded to Dad. "Hello, Sam's dad."

"Hello, Sam's friend," said Dad, dead serious. He likes Felix. "Sam, I'll pick you up after tea, OK?"

We waved him off all the way to the car.

"Goodbye . . . goodbye . . . going . . . going . . . gone!" Felix shut the door and turned to me. "Now what?"

We went to Felix's bedroom. It's on the ground floor, like mine, and it looks like a proper teenage room. The walls are painted black and covered with postcards and posters of rock groups with floppy black hair and piercings. The door has yellow hazard tape stuck across it and a sign that says "DANGER: UNEXPLODED BOMB".

I always feel weird in Felix's room. I thought about my room, with the blue furniture and the three shelves of books and the windowsill with the ship-in-a-bottle and my best Warhammer models and bits of quartz and fossils from Robin Hood's Bay. Felix is two school years ahead of me and he's supposed to be at secondary school. But I'm eleven and he's thirteen. That's not much older.

"What?" said Felix. He was watching me.

"Nothing," I said. Then, "I was just thinking about my list. 'Be a teenager'." I hesitated. "It was a stupid one to put."

"Pretty hard without a time machine," Felix agreed. "And who would waste a time machine on being a teenager?" He looked across at me and laughed. "Cheer up! The most important bit is doing the things, really, isn't it? Go drinking and smoking and have a girlfriend." He fumbled in the pocket on his chair and began pulling things out. A mobile phone, a fistful of Starburst wrappers and a map of Newcastle.

"What're you doing?" I asked suspiciously.

"Making all your wishes come true," said Felix. He found a crumpled pack of cigarettes and pulled one out. "Here."

I took the cigarette from him and held it between my first two fingers, the way smokers do. Felix leaned forward and lit it. I hesitated, then put it to my mouth and sucked. It tasted of hot and bitter and smoke. I held the smoke in my mouth for as long as I could stand it, to make sure it properly counted, and then blew it out again, coughing and spluttering. Felix was grinning.

"Like it?" he said.

"It's all right," I said awkwardly. "Where. . .? " I waved the cigarette around, looking for somewhere to put it out.

"Don't you want the rest?" said Felix.

"I'm OK," I said. I was going to say smoking gives you cancer, then I realized what a stupid thing it was to say. Felix ground the cigarette out on the arm of his wheelchair. He doesn't actually smoke very often. He just likes the way it looks.

"Come on, then," he said. "Pass us my coat – there – you're sitting on it. *There*." I didn't move. "Come *on*," he said again.

"Where're we going?"

"To do the other things, of course," he said impatiently. "Hurry up, though. Before Mum comes and finds us something else to do."

We set off down the street. I pushed Felix, who directed.

"Turn left. Cross over. Come on, fast! Faster! Can't you go any faster than *that*?"

He was having great fun not telling where we were going. All he would say was, "Don't ask questions. Wait and see."

I couldn't remember when I was last out on my own, without some grown-up fussing around. Felix's mum hadn't seemed to mind us going out.

Felix just said, "We're going to the Angel. We'll be back for tea."

And she said, "All right, then. You'll look after this young lad of mine for me, won't you, Sam?"

And I said, "Sure."

Felix's streets were older than mine. All the houses look the same where I live. The houses there were terraced and they all looked different, because the people living in them had painted their doors bright red or put up hanging baskets or new bay windows.

"Stop!" cried Felix.

We slithered to a halt outside a scruffy little pub on the corner. It was called the Avenging Angel. The paint on the door was chipped and peeling. It was shut.

"It's shut," I said.

"I know that," said Felix. "My uncle runs it. Knock there."

There was a white pub door and, by it, a blue house door. I knocked on the blue one. A girl younger than me answered. She had thick, wavy brown hair. She was wearing a little tartan skirt and black tights.

"What do you want?" she said.

"That's friendly," said Felix. "Honestly, we come all this way. . ." He shook his head. "I want to show Sam the Angel. Can I? Or is Uncle Mick around?"

"He's upstairs," she said. "And I'm not supposed to take people round the bar."

"Isn't she lovely?" said Felix. "Sam, this is my cousin Kayleigh. Kayleigh, this is my friend Sam from hospital."

Kayleigh peered at me. "What's wrong with you?" she said.

I didn't really want to go into it. "I've got spheroidal globules," I told her.*

Kayleigh looked at Felix uncertainly.

"Ignore him," said Felix. "Are you going to let us in the pub or what?"

"All right!" said Kayleigh. She tossed her head like she was really angry with us. "All right! But I'm blaming you if Dad catches us." She disappeared. She was back a minute later in what looked like her dad's trainers, with a great big jangly ring of keys to open the pub with.

Inside the Angel, it was like she was the landlady and we were the customers. She flicked on all the lights and then went and sat behind the bar on one of those high stools you get in pubs. I stood awkwardly behind Felix, holding on to the handles of his chair. I wasn't sure what I was supposed to do.

Felix, of course, was right at home.

"Can't you serve us something, Kayleigh?" he said. "Sam wants to know what it's like going out drinking. Haven't you got anything interesting we could have?"

Kayleigh sat up, all professional.

"We've got lots of things," she said. "There are loads of bottles Dad never uses all along the top shelf. D'you want one of them?"

*It's true. Leukaemia was invented by this guy John Hughes Bennett in 1845. The first kid diagnosed with leukaemia was in 1850. Dr Bennett looked at her blood through a microscope and said it was full of "colourless, granular, spheroidal globules". That was the white blood cells, only he didn't know it then.

The reason it took so long to diagnose a kid was that they didn't used to let kids go to hospital because they thought they carried infections. How weird is that?

"Depends what it is," I said cautiously.

Kayleigh pushed the barstool up against the back wall and knelt on top of it.

"Crème de menthe . . . that's mint . . . crème de cacao . . . that's coffee, I think, or chocolate . . . cherry brandy. . ."

"That's cherry," said Felix unhelpfully. "That's nice – have some of that one."

I would never go into someone else's pub and start serving them drinks, but Kayleigh was as fearless as Felix. She poured a drizzle of cherry brandy into two shot glasses for us, and the mint one in another for her.

"Go on, then," said Felix, reaching up for his cherry brandy.

I took the shot glass and sniffed at it. Then I took a sip. It wasn't much like cherries. It was sweet and sticky and tasted of alcohol, like Christmas wine. There was only enough in the shot glass for a mouthful and then it was gone.

"Well?" said Felix.

"Yeah," I said.

"That's two teenage things down," said Felix. He looked up at Kayleigh, who was sucking the last drops of alcohol off her fingers. "And one to go."

I knew exactly what he was thinking.

"No!" I said.

"What?"

"No way!"

"Oh, shut up." Felix leaned forward in his chair. "Hey,

Kayleigh."

Kayleigh was sprawled over the bar, pretty much lying on top of it. She looked down at Felix with her hair falling all over her face. "Yes, sir."

"If I dared you to do something, would you do it?"

Kayleigh giggled. "No!"

"Oh, go on. Don't be a child."

Kayleigh righted herself, looking cautiously at us through the falling strands of hair. "It depends what it is."

"You've got to kiss Sam. Properly. On the mouth."

"Felix!"

Kayleigh started giggling.

"This is nothing to do with me," I told her. "It's all his idea."

"Shut *up*. Will you do it, Kayleigh?"

Kayleigh went pink. "No! I mean, no! Not with you watching!"

It took Felix about ten minutes to get her out from behind the bar. She kept giggling and going, "No, but –" and covering her face with her hands. I stood there looking embarrassed.

"OK," said Felix, at last. "OK. Kayleigh. Stop laughing. Get on with it."

Kayleigh was bright red by this point. "You aren't allowed to look," she said.

"I'm not!"

"I *mean* it. You have to turn right round."

"I am! Look!"

"All right." Kayleigh and I stood there, not looking at each other. I wondered if she was expecting me to do something and, if so, what it was. I moved forward. She looked up then and smiled. She came right up to me, and kissed me, awkwardly.

On the mouth.

LIST No. 5 WAYS TO LIVE FOREVER

1. Say every morning: "I will say this again tomorrow."

2. Become a vampire. Hope you don't meet Buffy.

3. Have your body frozen. Then, in hundreds of years, when they've found a cure for cancer and the secret to eternal life, they'll unfreeze you. (With any luck, you'll get to meet robots and aliens and have your own private space shuttle too.)

4. Find the Fountain of Eternal Youth. Have a drink.
   (This way, you get to stay young.)

5. Copy your brain on to a disk and live on a computer.
   Hope you don't get a virus.

6. Find a Greek goddess and make her fall in love with you.
   Have her get Zeus the king of the gods to make you
   immortal. *

7. Make a Philosopher's Stone. (You not only get to live forever, you get unlimited gold as well.)

8. Find a girl called Eva and marry her. Then, even if you can't live forever, at least you can live for Eva.

* Just make sure she asks for eternal youth too. This happened to one guy in Greek Mythology who fell in love with the goddess of dawn. She asked Zeus to make him immortal but forgot about humans getting old, so he carried on getting crinklier and wrinklier forever and ever. So now that's why Dawn gets up so early every morning, because she has to share a bed with this shrivelled-up little old man.

GOING TO THE MOON

After we'd said goodbye to Kayleigh, me and Felix went and bought Refresher bars at the corner shop and sat and ate them in the park.

"Well?" said Felix. "Was it gross?" But I wouldn't tell him.

"We're getting there, you know," said Felix "Airships, being famous and space – that's it, right?"

"Yes," I said. "Is that what we're doing next, building a rocket?"

"Why not?" said Felix. He was sitting on the swing, legs dangling. He leaned back as far as he could. "We can do anything!" he shouted. "Anything!"

I started swinging, as high as I could. I was tired, but I hadn't felt as happy as this in ages. "We're going to the Moon!" I shouted.

It's mad, I know. But who knows? Maybe we could.

THE STORY OF STARS

Do you know where we came from? True fact: we came from stars.

When old stars die, they explode in this gigantic explosion, which makes a nebula. Nebulas are clouds of gas and dust. That's where baby stars grow. All the gas and dust gets compressed, gravity sucks them in and they turn into stars. The bits that don't turn into stars float around in space as planets or moons or comets, and if the conditions are right, plants and stuff start to grow and people are born. So we're all made of bits of old star. But it's a cycle. Because after millions of years the new star gets old and tired too and it explodes and more baby stars get born. If the old stars didn't die, you'd never get new ones.

Here's another true fact. Carbon, hydrogen, oxygen and nitrogen are the elements you need for life. And if you look at comets, you see that they have pretty much the same proportion of these elements as we do.

EXPLOSIONS   2nd February

I asked Mrs Willis about rockets today. "Could we build one, a
proper one? Would it count as school?"

"Anything counts as school if you try hard enough," she said.
"Rockets are clearly science. What do you want one for?"

"To go up in space," I said.

"Ah," she said. "Slightly harder. That probably comes
under . . . um . . . imaginative learning."

"Does that mean no?" I said.

"It means, don't tell health and safety," said Mrs Willis. "And
don't expect the education authority to pay. They can barely keep
me in lighter fluid."

We had a good lesson. We did "Making Fireworks", which really meant throwing iron filings and things into the burner on the cooker and watching them explode. Mrs Willis likes an explosion as much as anyone.

The only thing was, Felix didn't turn up.

Mum rang Felix's mum after lunch. She stayed out in the hall for ages. Then she came and sat at the table and watched me without saying anything. I was doing a tracing of a supernova.

"Sam. . ." she said.

"What happened to Felix?" I said.

Mum wouldn't answer properly. "Well," she said. "That's kind of what I want to talk to you about."

I looked up. Mum's face was serious. She was twisting the cuff of her jumper, turning it round and round and round.

"What?" I said. "*Mum*. What?"

She took a deep breath. "Sam, Felix went into hospital this morning."

I stared. I didn't know what to say. "But he can't!" I thought.

"Why?" I said.

"An infection, Gillian said. She's up there now."

Gillian is Felix's mum.

I was still staring. I didn't expect this to happen. It was like a small pit had opened in my stomach. I mean, I knew Felix was pretty ill, like me, but I didn't expect him to actually *get* ill.

"He'll be all right," I said.

Mum didn't say anything.

"He'll be fine," I said.

SUPERNOVA

This is a tracing of a supernova, which is a star exploding. A supernova is the bit where it actually explodes, not the bit where new stars and alien races are created.

KIDNAPPING THE PHONE   4th February

Two whole nights have gone by. Felix is still in hospital. I tried asking Annie if she knew anything when she came to give me platelets, but she said she didn't. Mrs Willis came again and asked me if I'd written any more book. I said no, even though I have. We just played Othello for school. I wish I'd never started writing a stupid book about getting ill. It doesn't seem funny any more. I wanted Mum to ring Felix's mum and find out what's happening, but she wouldn't. She said Gillian had enough to worry about without us bothering her.

I said, "What about me? *I'm* worried. At least she's *there*. Can't we go see him?"

Mum said, "*No*." She said, "He's very poorly, Sam. He wouldn't want you there. And we wouldn't want you catching anything, would we?"

I wanted to scream. That's so *unfair*. It's one thing to say nobody can go, but to say only I can't because it'd make me ill is *horrible*. Anyway, it doesn't make sense. You'd think I'd have *more* resistance to infections, not less, with my mega-reinforced resistance army of white blood cells.

I said, "That's discrimination! And anyway, people are only infectious when they first get ill, they aren't later." (I wasn't *entirely* sure this was true, but I said it anyway.) "And he would want me there, he *would*. He *said* so."

Mum said, "Sam. . ." She reached out her arm. I pulled away.

"No!" I shouted. "It's not *fair*!"

Mum sighed. "No," she said wearily. "It's not, but that's the way things are and you're just going to have to live with it."

"*No!*" I shouted. I pushed her. Then I ran out into the hall and slammed the door. I picked up the phone and started dialling. I don't know Felix's mum's mobile, but I know their home number.

Mum came after me and saw what I was doing. She grabbed for the phone. I pulled it away as far as the cord would go. The phone fell off the table and landed on the floor with a clunk. At the other end, I could hear a sleepy voice saying, "Hullo? . . . Hullo?"

"Mickey!" I said. "Mickey—"

Mum yanked the receiver off me. "Mickey, I'm so sorry—"

"Ask him!" I begged. "Ask him!"

Mum took the phone through into the living room. I followed. "*Sam!*" she said. "Mickey, I'm terribly sorry about this, but Sam's been so worried—"

I am an expert at eavesdropping, but even I couldn't tell much from Mum's "Right"s and "Of course"s. I had to sit there squirming until she put down the phone and glared at me.

"Well?" I said.

Mum opened her mouth like she was about to shout and then shut it again. "He's still in hospital," she said.

"And?"

"And he's still very poorly." She hesitated, then she said, "Mickey says he'll tell his mum we rang, but he said there isn't really much point in visiting him. He's sleeping a lot, he said."

I didn't say anything.

"His dad's coming up tomorrow, but they're not sure when he's going to get in. Sam—"

I didn't want to hear whatever she was going to say.

"He was all right on Saturday," I said. I couldn't get over how unfair it all was. "There wasn't anything wrong with him!"

THE STORY OF THE CURE

This is a story that I made up.

It starts with me at home. I'm cross and miserable. Mum's cross too. We're fighting. Mum's crying.

It seems as if nothing good is ever going to happen again.

And then the phone rings.

On the other end of the phone is Annie. She's very excited. A team of scientists has found a new drug, which has cured leukaemia in lots of laboratory hamsters and mice. All the laboratory hamsters and mice were lying there, about to die, but after they were given this drug they got better and now they're living happy lives as pets of the scientists' children.

The scientists need some human beings to test this drug on. They ring our hospital and talk to Annie.

"We need lots of people with leukaemia," they say. "Give us your sickest patients. The sicker the better. This drug is so good, they'll just take one *sniff* and they'll be disco dancing."

"Right you are," says Annie. And straight away she rings up all her patients and tells them about the scientists.

Some of the patients are doubtful.

"No way," they say.

"He's having us on."

"No drug can be *that* good."

But I say I'll give it a go.

The next day the scientists come round to our house. They give me a packet of little red-and-white striped pills.

"Here you go," they say. "This is it. Take two a day with a drink – whatever type you like best."

The drug is very good. As soon I have taken one pill I start to feel better. After I have taken two pills, I stop feeling tired. And after *three* pills I get up and start jumping on my bed. I run all around the house. I get out my bike and ride it up the hill and back down. I play basketball with Ella on the old hoop on our house and I beat her thirty-eight hoops to six.

After I have taken all the pills in the packet I am completely cured. The scientists are delighted. I am on the *World News*. All the newspapers in the world have pictures of me coming down our hill on roller blades and visiting other children with leukaemia to tell them about the pills.

The scientists make billions of pounds selling their pills to hospitals.

They give some of the money to me and I go on a world cruise with my family and Felix and Granny.

And no one ever dies of leukaemia. Ever again.

A PHONE CALL   5th February

Felix's mum rang the next evening.

You could see Mum jump when the phone rang. She'd already jumped for Grandma-in-Orkney and a man selling kitchens. She shut the living-room door again, so me and Ella couldn't hear what she was saying. I hate secrets and so does Ella. We looked at each other. Ella's face was white and her eyes were huge. We would have listened anyway, but Dad was there and he turned the news right up so we couldn't hear. Dad hadn't said anything about Felix being in hospital.

Not a thing.

We heard Mum's voice stop in the hall. There was a long,

grippy silence. Then she came back in and sat on the edge of the sofa. She was wearing her serious look again. All of a sudden, I didn't want to know.

"Was it Felix's mum?" said Ella.

"Yes," said Mum. She hesitated. "Sam, Gillian says – if you want to – she thinks maybe you should come and say . . . come and see him."

"Is he awake?" I said.

"No," said Mum. "Not really." She rubbed her hand across her leg. "Oh, I don't know," she said. "You don't have to if you don't want to."

I didn't want to.

Yes, I did.

No, I didn't.

"Yes," I said. "I'll go."

QUESTIONS NOBODY ANSWERS NO. 4

Does it hurt to die?

WHAT HAPPENED

It felt weird being back on our ward again. The nurse on the nurses' station was new and didn't recognize us. She said Felix had a private room. I trailed the tips of my fingers along the corridor walls as I followed Mum, remembering. Felix always used to say the sicker you got, the better service they gave you. Once, him and me emptied a whole bottle of vampire blood over his sheets to try and get this student nurse to bring us a bottle of Coke from the machine. She went *absolutely* white and screamed for one of the proper nurses to come. We didn't half get told off.

And she never got the Coke for us.

"There you are!"

I jumped. It was Mickey, Felix's brother, smiling at me and Mum over two cups of plastic hospital tea. He looked the same as always: big and rumpled, like a sleepy bear, with what looked like egg yolk down his T-shirt. He started talking to Mum. I listened at first, in case they said anything about Felix, but they just went on about his dad and his grandparents and someone else I'd never heard of. I stopped listening. I went and stood by his door, wanting to go in but not daring.

I felt sick.

When we finally did go in, it wasn't as bad as I'd thought it would be. Felix was lying in bed, on his back, in ordinary pyjamas. He looked asleep. His mum was sitting by the bed, holding his hand. She turned when we came in. She and Mum stared at each other, over the bed.

Then her face seemed to crumple and she burst into tears.

Me and Mum and Mickey just stood there in the doorway. I didn't know what to do. I'd never seen Felix's mum cry before. Maybe Mum had, though. She went right over to her and put her arms around her.

"Shh. . ." she said. "Shh . . . It's all right. It's all right." With her arm around her shoulder, she guided her towards the door, still talking in the same quiet voice. "Come on. Come on, now. Let's go somewhere quiet." And just like that, they were gone.

"It's all right," said Mickey. "There's a special room to flap in."

"I know," I said. I suddenly remembered what Felix had said, that he didn't want his mum to be there when he died, in case she got upset. I looked quickly at him. He hadn't moved.

"Would you like to come sit by him?" said Mickey. I nodded. He gave me a little push towards the chair.

"Hold his hand if you want. And talk to him. Let him know you're here."

"Can he hear?"

"Maybe."

I wondered if he was in a coma or just asleep. Probably a coma, I thought. You can't hear people when you're asleep. I wondered what would happen if I shook him and yelled, "Wake up!"

Maybe he'd open his eyes and shout, "Where's my Coke, then?"

Maybe not.

I sat in the chair but I didn't hold his hand. I felt very silly, sitting there. I know it was awful, but I couldn't help it. I wondered if he *could* see us, or hear us. If he could, I bet he was laughing at me.

"Hello," I said.

I couldn't think of anything else to say. Not with Mickey there. But Mickey seemed to understand. He said, "I'd better give Mum her tea. Would you like a cup?"

"Yes," I said. "Please."

"You'll be all right on your own, won't you?" he said. "You won't be frightened?"

"No," I said.

I wasn't frightened. He was just Felix.

He looked just like he was asleep.

What happened next was something incredible.

Something I didn't tell Mickey or Felix's mum or anyone.

Something secret.

I felt better after Mickey had gone. I sat in my chair looking at Felix, scuffing the soles of my trainers across the floor. It was quiet. Nice. Just the two of us.

"I wish you'd hurry up and wake up," I said. I knew he wasn't going to, really, but I still said it.

And then he opened his eyes.

He was looking right at me. I stared at him. I didn't know what to do. I thought maybe I should shout for Mickey, but I couldn't move. It was like he wanted me to do something, or say something, and I didn't know what.

"It's all right," I said.

He kept on looking. Then, suddenly, he smiled. More than smiled. He *grinned*, a big, wide, face-splitting grin. He looked so pleased that I found myself smiling back, without meaning to.

And then his eyes closed and his body relaxed.

I sat there on my black plastic hospital chair, by the bed, next to him. I knew I ought to go and get Mickey or a nurse or someone, but I didn't. I just sat there, quiet and close beside him, until they all came back.

WHAT IS DYING?

Death: The final cessation of vital functions in an organism; the ending of life.

The Concise Oxford Dictionary, Ninth Edition

When someone dies it means their body no longer works. Their heart stops beating, they no longer need to eat or sleep and they do not have any pain. They do not need their bodies any longer (which is good because their body doesn't work). Because dead people do not need their bodies we can no longer see them like we used to do before they died.

Children and Death by Danai Papadatou and
Costas Papadatos

ALONE IN THE NIGHT

I didn't sleep much the night Felix died. I felt very, very tired, but I didn't sleep. I stayed awake and listened. I listened to the central heating making noises. I listened to the rain pattering on the roof. I followed the familiar shapes of the shadows and tried to remember what each one was. *That* was my notice board, stuck up with all my cards. *That* was a laundry basket, full of clothes waiting to be put away. I lay awake and tried to breathe it in and save it up somewhere where I would remember it always.

Very late at night, I heard footsteps creaking down the stairs and my door opened. It was Ella. She was holding her big stuffed elephant and crying. I sat up in bed and looked at her. She didn't say anything. I think she was half asleep still. She padded over to the bed and sort of patted me, as if making sure I was still there. Then she climbed into bed beside me, wrapped her arms round the elephant and closed her eyes.

She's never done anything like that before.

I lay for a while pressed up against the wall, feeling her cold toes against my leg and the soft warmth of her body through her pyjamas. Then something seemed to relax inside me, and I closed my eyes and slept.

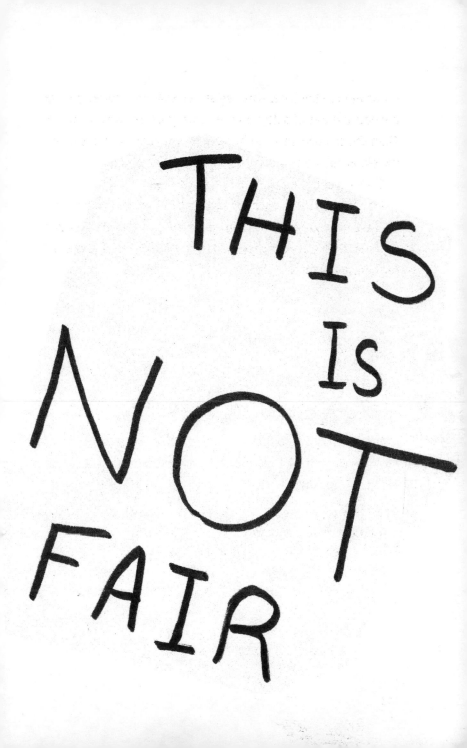

MUM   8th February

I stayed in bed the next day. I wrote and wrote and wrote. I didn't get up. Outside was grey and cold and full of rain. Annie came in the morning, but Mrs Willis didn't. Mum kept putting her head round the door and saying, "Are you all right?" or "Don't you want something to eat?"

I felt strange and heavy and not quite there. My bones were hurting again.

Mum kept looking like she wanted to say something and then not. I didn't want to talk to her. I didn't know what to say.

I could see she had been crying. Her face was red and watery and full of tears.

That evening, she came and sat by my bed.

"Sam. . ." she said. "Sam, do you think you could eat something? For me?"

I shook my head. My insides were all churned up, as if I was on a ship that wouldn't stay still, as if the whole world was a ship, rocking and swaying in a storm. Mum nodded once or twice. She took a deep, shuddering breath.

"Maybe you could have some milkshake. . ."

She went away and made me some milkshake. I held the glass, awkwardly. It felt smooth and heavy between my fingers. The skin on my hand felt tender and numb at the same time. I could feel every prickle of my jersey against my arms and my neck.

Mum was looking at me.

"Please," she said.

I drank about half of the milk. And then I was sick, all over the duvet and down my jersey.

Mum just sat there looking at me.

I began to shake. I couldn't stop myself. And then I realized I was crying, although whether it was because of Felix, or because I'd been sick, or because I felt so tired and ill, I don't know.

Mum reached out and put her arm around me but I cried out, because it hurt. So then she took her arms away and she was crying too.

"I hate it," I said. My voice came out in this high squeak, all shaken up with sobs. "I hate it. I *hate* it."

Mum nodded. Her face was shiny with tears.

"So do I," she said. "Oh, love. So do I."

I can't remember how long we cried for. But I do remember when we were finished she gave me some tissue and I rubbed my face with it and she dried her eyes. And I could see how much she wanted to make it all right again, but she couldn't. So she went and got a new duvet cover and helped me put on a clean T-shirt. And she brought me a night light on a saucer and turned out the big light so that there was just this one little circle of candlelight on my bedside table. And then she sat there on the chair, beside the bed, beside me, until I fell asleep.

LIST NO 6 WHAT TO DO WHEN SOMEONE DIES

1. When a Hindu dies, his family lights a small flame, which sits in the house beside his body. Hindus believe that when someone's soul first leaves his body, it is confused and doesn't know where to go. The flame gives it somewhere to live. After ten days, the flame is carried to the sea and put in the water. This tells the spirit it is time to start the journey to the afterlife

2. Pygmies don't like death. When someone dies they pull his hut down on top of him, move the camp away and never talk about him again.

3. Jamaicans celebrate for nine nights after someone dies. They put food out for the dead person, dance, sing and drink very strong rum.

4. When a Jewish person dies they are washed by men or by women, depending on which one they are, and dressed in a white shroud. Their body is never left alone until it is buried. This is a way of respecting the dead person and

making sure that the body isn't stolen. At the funeral, people tear their clothes, to show their grief. Afterwards, they all sit in shiva, which means mourning.

5. Mexicans have a big party. It's called the Days of the Dead and it happens on the first and second of November. They go and visit people's graves and decorate the country with skulls and skeletons. They cook food for their dead relatives and set places for them at the table.

6. Some Alaskan Inuits used to cover dead bodies with an igloo. It is so cold in Alaska that the body would stay frozen forever, unless polar bears ate it.

I woke late next morning. I lay on my side and listened to the noises of my family. Ella was watching Saturday morning cartoons. I could hear the muffled noise of the television and Ella laughing. Mum was in the kitchen, clattering about with the pans. She was listening to Radio Four and talking to Dad. I could hear their conversation but not what they were saying; just the old, familiar sounds of their voices, rising and falling, as if from underwater or from a long, long way away.

"This is what it'll be like when I'm gone," I thought. I felt half gone already, lying there behind my door. I was very tired. I thought about Felix. Felix, locked in a box and dropped down a hole. I closed my eyes.

I don't know how long I'd been lying there when someone knocked on the door.

"Come in," I said.

Ella opened the door and stood there, looking at me.

"Are you all right?" she said.

"Yes," I said.

She came in a little further.

"You don't look all right," she said.

She was standing on one foot in the doorframe, her dark hair all about her face. She looked so pink and solid I wanted to hit her. "Lemme alone," I said. "I'm fine. Go away."

"I'm getting Mum," she said, and she vanished. I moaned and buried my head in my pillow. I didn't want to face Mum again.

I heard someone come into the room and felt the bed move as they sat down beside me. I kept my head in the pillow.

"Sam?" Mum said. "Sam? Are you all right, love?"

"I'm *fine*!" I said, into my pillow.

Mum smoothed my hair off my forehead. I jerked my head away.

"Did that hurt?"

"No!" I said.

She touched my shoulder. I cried out.

Mum sighed. "Maybe we should call Annie—"

"Leave me alone!" I shouted. And then, because I knew she was going to argue, "I want to go and see Felix."

Mum drew in her breath. For a moment, she didn't say

anything. Then she said, "I don't know that that's a very good idea."

"I want to," I said.

"I know you do. But . . . it can be quite upsetting, seeing someone who's dead. And you're really not very well. Wouldn't it be better just to remember him like he was?"

"No," I said. "No!" I turned my head away. All the time I was thinking, 'Why can't I see him? What does he look like? What's wrong with him?'

"You've got to let me see him," I said. "It'll make me worse, if you don't let me."

Mum drew a deep breath.

"Sam," she said. She was almost pleading. "Let's not fight. Please. Not now."

"I'm not fighting," I said. "*You're* the one fighting. If you'd let me go, we wouldn't have to fight."

Mum's face was very pale. Her lips were pressed in a pink line.

"Well," she said. "If that's what you want to think, then you go on thinking that. I'm not going to argue with you."

I hated her then. *Hated* her. Hated her for the tight, unhappy look that I knew was my fault. Hated her for not letting me win. Hated her because I was terrified of what might have happened to Felix, of what no one ever told me.

"You have to do what I say," I said, furious. "Everyone has to. Because I'm going to die and then you'll be sorry."

Mum sat perfectly still, pressing her lips together. For a

moment, neither of us moved. Then she turned and ran out of the room.

I clenched my teeth and buried my head in my pillow. Good, I thought. Good. Serves her right. But I didn't feel any happier.

I just felt miserable. And angry. And lonely.

I lay in bed for a long time, listening. I heard Ella's urgent voice. "What's the matter? Mum? Mum? What's the matter?"

I heard Mum and Dad talking, and Mum crying, on and on. I think I must have fallen asleep, because then I heard Granny's voice and I don't remember the doorbell ringing.

"Oh, for pity's sake!" That's what she said, very loud. And then, "Well, why shouldn't he, if he wants to?" And then there was Dad, murmuring something.

After a while, Granny came into my room and sat on the edge of my bed.

"Your mother's talked to Gillian," she said. "She says you can go and see Felix this afternoon, if you're well enough."

"I'm well enough," I said.

She made a sort of tutting noise. "You'll have to do better than that, my lad," she said. "You look like the baby who was washed down the plughole with the bath water. Why don't you have something to eat, and then we'll see?"

I'd pushed myself up on my elbows, but when she said that, I flopped back down again on the bed.

"I'm not hungry," I said. I wasn't. I didn't feel sick any more, but sort of empty, as though my stomach had shrivelled up inside me. Granny looked at me.

"We don't want any of that," she said. "Your poor mother's worried sick about you. She's got enough on her plate, without you playing her up."

This was so unfair that I sat right up.

"I'm not!" I said.

Granny gave a brisk nod. "That's more like it," she said. "I'll go and find you some food."

QUESTIONS NOBODY ANSWERS No. 5

What does a dead person look like?
Or feel like?

BULLET HOLES 9th February

Granny took me to the funeral place herself, in her gardening van. There's only room for one person besides Granny and they always get to sit in the front. The rest of the van is full of spades and netting and big sacks of sand. It has the bullet holes that I got Granny for Christmas stuck on the windscreen. It rattles when you drive too fast.

Granny always drives too fast.

It took us ages to get there, even so. All the way, I got nervouser and nervouser. My nervousness grew like a balloon under my ribs. It tingled down my arms and made my heart beat and beat, until I felt like I was going to burst.

When we finally got there, the funeral place didn't look at all like I thought it would. It was very posh. It looked a bit like the reception at Dad's work. There was a pink carpet and a desk with a lady in a dark blue suit and pictures of flowers in pink frames on the wall. When Granny told the lady Felix's name, she led us down this big long corridor with lots of shiny doors off it. I edged closer to Granny. She gave me a smile.

I wondered if it was too late to change my mind.

At last, the lady stopped outside one of the doors and unlocked it.

"Here you are," she said to Granny. "Let me know when you're ready to leave."

Granny nodded. "Right," she said. The lady smiled and set off back down the corridor. "Thank you!" Granny called after her. She turned and waved her hand.

Me and Granny looked at each other.

"Still time for an honourable retreat," she said.

I shook my head.

"Sure?"

I nodded. She squeezed my shoulder.

"Good man," she said and opened the door.

The room was small and very plain. There were white walls, another picture of pink flowers and a sort of bed with Felix on it. Granny went over to the bed, quietly. I hung back. She didn't say anything, to me or him. She just stood there, looking. I edged closer, slowly, until I stood right beside her. Then I looked too.

Felix was lying on his back. He was dressed in his old Green Day T-shirt, all streaky from too much washing, and his black French resistance beret. He looked exactly like Felix, just exactly as if he were sleeping, except he was too stiff and still to be asleep. He looked cleaner and neater than he ever did in real life. His eyes were closed.

I reached out and touched his shoulder, on the T-shirt. Then I touched him properly, on the jaw, on the skin.

He was very cold. Not cold like fingers in the snow are cold, still warm under the skin. Stone cold, like statues of old knights in cathedrals. With no warmth left in them at all.

I realized I'd been hoping, somehow, that they'd made some sort of mistake. They might have done. But now as I stood there, I knew there hadn't been any mistake. He was so still and quiet. He looked exactly like Felix, but there wasn't any *person* left in him at all. Wherever he was now, it wasn't here.

I'd thought he'd be frightening. He wasn't. He was just quiet and empty.

I fell asleep again on the way back, curled up on Granny's front seat with my feet on a bag of tulip bulbs. I was so, so tired. I slept all the way home. When I woke, it was evening. I was in my own bed, Granny had gone and it was raining.

THE STORY OF THE MAN WHO
WEIGHED THE HUMAN SOUL

This is a story I read in a book. It's true. In 1907, a surgeon called Dr Duncan MacDougall decided to find out how much a human soul weighed. So he made a special bed on a set of scales. He put one of his patients on the bed and weighed him while he was dying. He said that the man got lighter very, very slowly, because of the sweat that was evaporating. But at last he died and CLUNK! the scales dropped. Dr MacDougall said that the moment the man died, he lost three-fourths of an ounce, or twenty-one grams.

When I heard this story I got out our kitchen scales to try and find out how much twenty-one grams really is. I was a bit disappointed. According to Dr MacDougall, the human soul weighs as much as four and a half pencils. Or three greetings cards.* Or a wooden letter opener, a sheet of stickers and a used-up glitter pen.

Which isn't very much.

Anyway. Dr MacDougall tried his experiment on three other patients. Once, the patient lost less weight than the first patient, and twice they lost some weight first and more weight later. Then Dr MacDougall tried the same thing with fifteen dogs and none of them got lighter at all. He said that this proved he was measuring the soul, because he didn't think dogs have souls. But there were lots of problems with his experiment. Often it's hard to tell exactly when someone has died. And six patients weren't enough to test it properly. And his scales weren't very accurate. And there could've been loads of reasons for what happened that he didn't know about.

But nobody since has been able to explain why they got lighter. It wasn't from water evaporating. And it wasn't because air had left their lungs, because Dr MacDougall tried breathing air in and out of the first man's mouth and it didn't change his weight. Sometimes they wet themselves, but that didn't matter because the wee stayed on the bed and was still being weighed.

Nobody has ever repeated his experiment (or if they have, I

*Yes, greetings cards are heavier than pencils. Try weighing them yourself and see.

couldn't find them on Google). I suppose most people don't want scientists weighing them while they're dying and nowadays you have to ask people before you do stuff to them.

So nobody knows. He was probably wrong.

But what if he was right?

What if he proved we have a soul?

ANNIE   10th February

When Annie came to give me platelets, she stood and talked to
Mum for ages. Then she came and talked to me.

I was curled up on the sofa with Columbus, watching *Pirates of the
Caribbean* and squeezing my platelets. Annie came and sat by me.

"Hey there," she said.

"Hey," I said. I didn't take my eyes off the television.

"Your mum says you've been a bit poorly."

"I'm fine," I said.

Annie didn't push it. "She says you went to see Felix."

I didn't answer.

"Do you want to talk about it?"

I stared at the television. Annie sat back on the sofa. We watched the film for a bit like it was all we cared about. I wasn't fooled. But there *was* something I wanted to ask her.

"Annie. . ."

"Mmm?"

"When they bury people . . . do they ever make mistakes? Like, bury people alive?"

Annie turned and looked at me. She said, "Oh no, Sam. Doctors are very careful. They always check pulse and blood pressure before they pronounce someone dead."

I squirmed. The cat mewed softly. "I know, but . . . what if they make a mistake?"

Annie reached out and stroked the cat. He was warm and heavy in my lap. "It's very hard to make a mistake, especially after someone has been dead for a couple of hours. Bodies behave very differently after death. They get very pale and cold. And the muscles stiffen – like zombies in cartoons."

I knew that really, from Felix. "But people wake up sometimes, don't they?" I said.

"Not after about fifteen minutes," said Annie. "Really, Sam. The brain can't survive that long without oxygen."

I nodded. "I did know really," I said. I yawned. "I just wanted to be sure."

On the television, the pirate skeletons were busy trashing the town. I leaned my head against Annie's shoulder and we watched it together.

QUESTIONS NOBODY ANSWERS NO. 6

Why do people have to die anyway?

THE FUNERAL

Felix's funeral was today. Mum, Ella and I went.

I'd never been to a funeral before, so I didn't know what to expect. I imagined people crying and everyone dressed in black. Felix would have liked that. He liked black. He'd have liked everyone gothed up with black eyeliner and black nail varnish. I wished we'd thought of it – just to see all his old relations do it.

We didn't wear black. Ella wore the floaty green skirt that she got for my cousin's wedding and sandals with bright orange flowers on them. Mum didn't want her to, but she wouldn't change.

"But Ella, you'll freeze in that big church."

"I don't care." Ella sat on Dad's chair and crossed her arms to show she wasn't going to be moved. "I want to wear something pretty." So she did.

And a duffle coat.

Dad didn't come. He just went off to work as usual. He didn't even sign the card we bought.

There were loads of people in the church. Most of them I didn't know, but some of them I did. There was Mickey and Felix's dad, who lives on a farm and has lots of hair and plays the didgeridoo, but not in church. There was Kayleigh, standing very close to her dad. And Dr Bill, all dressed up. Even Mrs Willis was there. She was over on the other side of the church, but she smiled specially at me when we came in. She wasn't wearing black either.

The funeral was very strange. Everyone sang hymns. Ella got very upset when they started. She said in this big loud voice, "But Felix didn't believe in God!"

"Ella!" hissed Mum.

"But he didn't!" Ella said.

"Shhh!" said Mum. She went pink. She glanced at the old lady sitting next to us, probably wondering if she was Felix's gran or something. "If you can't behave yourself, I'm taking you out."

"But—" said Ella.

The old lady leaned across Mum. "It's a silly nonsense, dear," she said to Ella. "But you can't say anything. You don't want the vicar to burst into tears, do you?"

Ella was so surprised to be spoken to by a stranger that she shut right up. But she didn't sing any of the hymns. Neither did I. Not because I thought it was a nonsense, but because Ella was right. Felix wouldn't have wanted hymns. He'd have wanted . . . Green Day or something. All his old relations singing Green Day. And then his dad playing the didgeridoo.

After the hymns, Felix's dad stood up and said some stuff. All about how brave and cheerful Felix was and how he never complained about things. Which wasn't true. Felix *was* brave, but he used to moan all the time when we were in hospital. We used to make plans about how we were going to drop grenades on all the nurses. And then Felix's dad started telling these stories about Felix as a little kid, which I suppose is when he knew him best, because he and Felix's mum still lived together then. It was all a bit stupid, though. Felix wasn't some cute kid. And he wasn't a child hero either. He got narky just like everybody else.

Ella didn't like Felix's dad's speech any better than she liked the hymns. She started drooping. She slid further and further down our bench, getting lower and lower until she slid right off the seat and on to the floor, where she didn't have to look at Felix's dad. Mum didn't know what to do. You could see half of her wanting to tell Ella off and the other half thinking that if she was hiding on the floor at least she wasn't saying any more rude things about the funeral.

Ella wrapped her arms around her legs and rested her head on her knees. She looked so sad and tired that I slid down off my bench too and sat on the floor beside her.

It was nice on the floor. We didn't have to look at the flowers or the coffin or all the horrible people in black suits. Ella turned her head round to look at me. Her face was white and her forehead had a red mark where she'd pressed it against her knee. Her little bare toes were white with cold.

"Felix would have thought this was stupid," I whispered to her. She gave me a tiny smile.

"We should've done the speech instead," I whispered. "'Felix was good at making jokes and messing about. He liked bossing people around and making everyone listen to him and having the last word.'"

Ella smiled. "'He liked jelly babies,'" she whispered. "'And arguing.'"

"'And *winning* arguments,'" I said. "'And doing things he wasn't supposed to. Like smoking cigarettes.'"

"'He was good at tickling,'" Ella said. I had a sudden picture of Felix in hospital, where we first met, with Ella crawling all over him and him tickling her until she screamed. I suddenly felt very tired.

"'He had lots of ideas,'" I said. "'And he made up lots of games. He never thought anything was impossible.'"

"'He could do anything,'" whispered Ella. She gave a little sigh. She leaned her head against my shoulder and closed her eyes.

THINGS THAT HAVE HAPPENED

I haven't written anything in this book for a while, but nothing has happened for ages. We went to see Auntie Nicola for a weekend. Mum's friends Sue and David came to stay and we went to Butterfly World.

Granny took me and Ella to see *Stig of the Dump*. Everything just kind of was.

Everything is still harder than it ought to be. Mum got very fussy about things like eating meals and wearing hats and scarves. Dad shouted at Ella for being mopey in Butterfly World and made her cry. It has been very wet and grey.

Today, though, something happened.

A SNOW FALL

When I woke up this morning, the whole world had changed. Even the sun was brighter. There were all these little coins of white light, dancing on my bedroom wall. And when I opened my curtains, I couldn't stop staring. Our street, the other houses, the garden; it was as if everything had been put through the wash and come out white and sparkling.

Mum and Dad and Ella were eating breakfast when I went through.

"It's snowed!" I said.

"We know," said Ella. She put her spoon in her mouth and sucked on it, peering at me over the top of it. "Stupid."

I ignored her. Ella has been really weird recently. Acting like a little kid or bursting into tears or fighting for no reason.

"Can we go sledging?" I said.

Mum looked me up and down. Then she said calmly, "I don't see why not."

Ella dropped her spoon into her bowl with a splash.

"Can I come too?"

"Don't be silly," said Dad. He didn't look up from his toast. "You've got to go to school."

Ella scowled at him. She lashed out with her foot and hit the table leg. Dad carried on eating as though she wasn't there. "That's so *unfair*!" Ella wailed.

"Yes," Mum said unexpectedly. "It is. Of course you can come, Ella."

"No, she can't." Dad looked up.

"Why not?" said Mum. She looked him squarely in the face, but her hand tightened on her spoon. "We might not get snow again this year. It will be good for us to have a day together while . . . while Sam's well."

I glanced quickly at Dad. He looked away. "We can't just drop everything," he said. You could see he didn't like talking like this. He took off his glasses and began polishing them with the tablecloth. "We still have to . . . to . . . I still have to go to work. . ."

"No, you don't," said Mum. Ella and I stared at her. Dad always goes to work. He even went when I was in hospital last year. It's what he does. To say he didn't have to was like saying we didn't have to eat, or wear clothes. "You have staff, don't you? You don't need to go in every day. In fact, there's no reason why you can't come sledging too."

"You are not going sledging!" Dad shouted. He slammed the flat of his hand down on the table. Ella and I flinched. "Sam's ill, for ... for God's sake! You oughtn't to take him out in this weather, anyway."

Ella's eyes were round and fearful. Mum and Dad hardly ever fight. And when they do, Dad doesn't shout. Mostly he just says, "We're not going to talk about this" and walks out of the room. And mostly Mum leaves it at that. I'd never seen her stand him down like this. It was like she was a different person.

I thought she was going to shout back, but she didn't. She was watching Dad with an odd look on her face. "Just exactly what difference do you think it's going to make?" she said. "Tell me that."

Dad's mouth moved but nothing came out. His eyes were darting about the room, from his glasses still on the table, to the family photograph on the wall, to me. They settled on me. He stared at me as if he had never seen me before. I stared back. I didn't know what to say.

"You see," said Mum, very gently.

"No," said Dad. He turned to Ella. "Ella, go and get your coat. I'm taking you to school."

"No-o-o!" Ella wailed.

"I'll take her," said Mum. She turned and marched out of the room. Ella slid off her chair and ran after her. I stood there awkwardly, watching. Dad finished his toast in silence while Ella and Mum banged about, getting their things together. Then the front door slammed and the house was silent.

There we were, just the two of us. Dad cleared his throat. I waited.

"You . . . you're all right, aren't you, Sam?" he said.

"Yes," I said. What else could I say?

"Of course you are," said Dad. He patted me clumsily on the shoulder. "Good boy. My good lad." He went to get his coat.

When he had gone, I sat at the table and wondered what was going to happen. I was still there when Mum came back. She peered round the door and put her finger to her lips.

"Has he gone?" she whispered.

"Yes," I said. She vanished. I followed, curious. Mum opened the front door. Ella was standing there in her duffle coat, with her school bag over her shoulder.

"Run and get dressed while I dig out the sledges," said Mum. She hesitated and then she smiled at me, a wide, sudden smile that I'd almost forgotten she had. It was as if the sun had come out. "And don't tell your dad."

I couldn't help worrying about Dad, all the way to the park in the taxi. I felt a bit like we'd betrayed him, going out in the snow when he'd said we weren't to. But I didn't know what else to do. Mum was right. This might be the last chance we got to go sledging. I couldn't not go.

But I still wished Dad had come too.

There was absolutely no one else on the sledging hill. Not even tiny children too small to go to school. I'd only ever been there before when it was covered in kids, and the emptiness was almost frightening. There was this queer, white, waiting feeling, as if the whole world was holding its breath.

"Who's going first?" said Mum. "Or both together?"

I couldn't believe she was actually letting me go down the hill. Normally she'd be all worried about me hurting myself or something. But I didn't argue. Me and Ella have got our own plastic sledge each. We both sat down on them together.

"One," said Mum. "Two. Three. Go!"

I pushed with my feet and jerked my whole body forwards, the way you do on a swing. The sledge wouldn't go at first and then, all of a sudden, it began to slide. Slowly at first, then faster. I could feel the wind against my cheeks. I could feel the cold through my gloves. I could see the hedge at the bottom of the hill and, beyond it, the long loop of the river. "I have never felt this alive," I thought. "Never. I want this to last forever." But then there was the hedge, coming closer and closer, and I stuck my feet out into the snow and the sledge stopped just in time and it was over. Ella slid down beside me. Her cheeks were flushed and her eyes shone.

"Again!" she said.

We dragged our sledges up the hill again. We went down feet first, face first, on our stomachs, on our backs, with the sky jolting and shaking above us, on one sledge together. We got warmer under our coats, and we took off our hats and scarves and gloves and left them in a pile by Mum. Mum stood at the top of the hill and watched us. She took photographs: me and Ella with our sledges, me and Ella going down the hill, me and Ella together. She even went down herself, on Ella's sledge, although she said once was enough.

"I'm too old for this," she said, laughing.

"Never!" said Ella and hugged her.

After a time, I got tired and my bones started hurting again, so I went and stood with Mum at the top of the hill, watching Ella. There were other people about now, a woman with two dogs and a grandad with a little boy on a sledge. Our beautiful white slope was all torn and scarred with sledge-tracks and footprints. I knew we couldn't help spoiling it, but I still wished we hadn't. It began to snow again.

"Ella!" called Mum. "Come on in now!"

We went to the park café with the glass roof and had hot chocolate, one each, with marshmallows. Ella slurped at hers and got a creamy moustache. I copied her, because she looked so silly. Mum smiled at us both. She got the waitress to take a photograph of the three of us. We sat together, not talking much.

"Felix would have liked this," said Ella, suddenly.

We looked at each other awkwardly.

"Yes," said Mum. She didn't seem to mind Ella talking about him. She smiled at me and squeezed my fingers across the table.

"He would."

Ella nodded and sipped her hot chocolate.

After a while, she got up and went to look at the old-fashioned coffee-shop posters behind the counter. Mum went to pay the bill. I stood by the glass wall and looked out over the park. The snow was really falling now, millions and millions of soft, feathery snowflakes swirling around and around, above and before me. I watched them falling. Settling on the sledge scars and the footprint holes. Smoothing out all of our damage and making everything clean and new again.

QUESTIONS NOBODY ANSWERS NO. 7

Where do you go after you die?

WHAT HAPPENED IN THE
MIDDLE OF THE NIGHT

Dad didn't say anything about sledging when he got home. Neither did Mum. They both acted like the morning hadn't happened.

I was curled up on the sofa with my big book about airships. The fire was on. Outside, dusk had settled over the piles of frozen snow on the grass. It was warm and quiet and sleepy.

Dad came and sat down on the sofa beside me. He didn't say anything. He opened his paper and stared at it. Then he shut it again.

"Do you want a game of penalties or something?" he said.

I stared at him. We haven't played penalties in ages. It was pitch dark outside and freezing.

"I don't really want to right now, Dad," I said. "I'm really tired."
He nodded once or twice. "I'm sorry."

"It's all right," he said. His eyes wandered around the room, the
way they had that morning. They settled on my airship book. He
cleared his throat. "There – there was something in the paper
about an airship they've got up in the Lake District. Do you want
to hear it?"

I nodded. He fumbled with the sails of paper, trying to find the
page he wanted. "There we are," he said.

He smoothed out the page and began to read.

That night, last night, I couldn't sleep. I kept having these dreams
and waking up and not knowing whether I was asleep or awake.
And my bones hurt. I didn't realize they were hurting at first; it
was so muddled up with dreaming and sleeping. But then I woke
up again and I was tangled up in my sheets and I was crying and
I couldn't work out why and then my dad was there.

It's usually Mum who comes. I didn't know why it was Dad
then. He came right over to my bed and he said "Sam! Sam, are
you all right?" but I just kept on crying and twisting about,
because I still couldn't really work out what was happening.

He put his hand on my arm and I lashed out and knocked his
glasses off his nose. He put his hands on my shoulders and he said,
"Sam. Sam. Wake up. Wake up. I'm here. Wake up," and then I *did*
wake up a bit and saw it was him. I stopped crying so much then.

He said, "What's the matter? Where does it hurt?" and I said, "Everywhere," and started crying again.

He looked sort of panicky then. He pulled open the door of my cabinet and began rummaging through it, looking for my tablets. There's loads of stuff in there: pills, injections, things I used to take and don't any more. Dad pulled more and more things out until there was a whole pile by the bed.

"It's a box," I said. "Mum had it before."

"I know it's a box!" Dad swore. I leaned over, out of the bed, and saw it, under some fake spit from when I was ill last time.

"Dad. *Dad*. . ."

He wasn't listening, as usual. He was still shuffling through all the bits with his hands. I tugged on his sleeve.

"*Dad*. There. . ."

He saw it. He snatched it up and began fumbling with the lid. The box burst open and all the pills fell out. Dad swore again.

"It's all right," I said. "Dad. It's all right." He stopped and looked up at me.

"Look at you," he said. "How about you be the dad and I'll be the kid, eh?"

I rolled back on to my pillow and smiled up at him. He still looked nervy. He said, "I'll get you some water for this. Don't go anywhere, eh?"

I shook my head.

He sat on my bed and watched me take my pill. When I'd finished, he took the glass back and placed it on the cabinet. I thought he'd go back to bed then, but he just sat there, looking down at me.

"Was that what all those tears were about, then?" he said.

I shook my head. "I was dreaming."

"Were you?" He reached across me and straightened my duvet. "What about?"

"Oh. . ." It didn't seem to matter now. "I can't remember."

"No. . ." He sat there silent.

"I was dreaming," he said. "That's why I woke up."

"What were you dreaming about?" I said sleepily.

He rubbed his chin. I thought he wasn't going to answer, or hadn't heard. I was too sleepy to care much. But then – "About you," he said. I turned my face towards him. He was quiet again. "You," he said. "Going away. . ."

I know I must have been half asleep. Because when I looked at him then, there were tears in his eyes.

"Dad. . ." I said. "Don't cry." I reached out my hand and touched his, a little frightened. "Dad."

He *was* crying. There were little snail-trail tear tracks running down his cheeks. I blinked at him, trying to work it out.

"Dad. . ."

"Sam," he said. He grasped my hand. He seemed about to say something else, but my eyes were already closing. I was floating away, back across the shadowy border and into sleep.

LIST NO.7 FIVE FACTS ABOUT DAD

This is a page me and dad wrote today. These are facts about my dad.

1. He is thirty-nine years old. He likes spaghetti and baked beans. He doesn't like anchovies.

2. His favourite word is orgulous, which means haughty or splendid. He is not very haughty or splendid, though.

3. He has a bald patch the size of a fifty-pence piece. He says this is my and Ella's fault.

4. When he was a little boy he wanted to be a mountain climber. He was going to climb Everest, but then he found out that Edmund Hillary had got there first. This is a picture of my dad when he was my age.

5. My dad's favourite joke is:
Where does Napoleon keep his armies? Up his sleevies.

Dad's cartoons

SURPRISES 4th March

I slept late again next morning. When I woke up, Dad was there.

"Dad!" I said.

"What?" he said. He put on a serious face. "Aren't I allowed to spend some time with my son?"

"Of course you are!" I said. I hugged him. He looked surprised, but pleased. He hugged me back. "What do you want to do?" he said.

We had a great morning. I didn't want any proper breakfast so we had tinned peaches and ice cream and grapes, in bed. Mum had gone to see Granny, and Ella was at school. Dad had taken a whole day off work just to see me. We played Top Trumps and

Risk in Mum and Dad's bed and I won.

Mrs Willis didn't come, but we did school. Dad told me the story of Loki, who stole Sif's hair in the night and then had to go and ask the dwarfs to make her some more. I'd forgotten how good Dad is at telling stories. He does voices and everything.

After Dad told his story, I read him the bit from my book about going up the down-escalators. He liked it so much that I read him the bit with the Ouija board as well. And some of the lists.

"Where did you find all this stuff?" he said.

"From the Internet," I said. "And books too. Mrs Willis brings books sometimes."

He was pretty impressed, so I showed him my "Things To Do".

"I've done nearly all of them," I told him. He looked so surprised that I laughed. I told him all about it. He didn't get upset. He just sat and listened.

"So there's just airships and spaceships left?" he said.

"And being a scientist," I said.

He raised his eyebrows. "Isn't that what this is?" he said, tapping my folder.

I hadn't thought of my book like that. Did all those arguments with Felix count as being a scientist? I wanted to ask Dad, but then Annie came round. She looked at the games and paper and books and breakfast things all over the bed, with Columbus curled up in the middle of them, and laughed.

"You look like you're having a party!" she said.

She gave Dad some stronger tablets for me to take. It was a

shame really because they made me so sleepy that I couldn't stay awake. Dad didn't mind. He let me stay in the big bed. I lay and watched him as he cleared away all the mess.

As he was about to go, I said, "Dad."

He turned. "What?"

I looked at him, standing there in the door, with his book of Norse myths under his arm and his glasses all askew. "Nothing," I said.

He looked at me. Then he came over to the bed and hugged me so tight I thought I was going to explode.

"Sleep well," he said.

I did. I slept all afternoon. Except once I woke up and thought I heard Dad talking on the phone.

"Yes, I knew that. But aren't there any other options?"

I thought he was talking to Dr Bill again. Then he said, "I wouldn't want to interrupt filming."

Filming?

"Yes, a short flight . . . No . . . No, really? Washing powder? . . . Well, it's worth a try . . . Yes . . . Yes, thank you."

He put the phone down. I lay there, wondering sleepily what was going on. Had I been dreaming? But I was so tired, it didn't seem very important. I closed my eyes and fell asleep again.

DAD'S AIRSHIP

Airship: A power-driven aircraft that is lighter than air.

Concise Oxford Dictionary: Ninth Edition

A Skyship 600

AN ADVERTISEMENT FOR
WASHING POWDER   5th March

Next morning, when Mum was getting Ella ready for school, the phone rang. Mum answered.

"Hello? . . .Yes . . . *Who*? . . . He said *what*?"

I rolled over in bed and craned round so I could peer through the open bedroom door.

"Daniel! I've got a man from a film company here. Says he talked to you yesterday!"

"Oh, yes. . ." Dad came through, still clutching a piece of toast. He took the phone from Mum, who gave him a funny look. "Hello? . . . Yes? . . . Yes. *Really?* That's wonderful! . . . Hang on . . . four p.m., Legburthwaite . . . Yes . . . Yes. Thank you very much . . .

Goodbye, now."

He put the phone down. Mum and Ella were staring. So was I.

"What," said Mum, "was that about?"

"Are you going to be in a film?" said Ella.

Dad laughed. "Of course I'm not going to be in a film," he said. He rubbed his hands together, like the conjuror about to pull the rabbit out of a hat. "That was a man called Stanley Rhode. He's doing some work for a company that's filming an advert up on Helvellyn."

"An *advert*?" said Mum.

Dad laughed again. "For washing powder," he said. "Can you believe it? I think they're going to spray the washing powder out from behind it and make some joke about clothes as clean as clouds."

"*Daniel!*" said Mum. "What *are* you talking about? Spray washing powder out of *what*?"

"Oh." Dad looked startled. "Didn't I say? From an airship, of course."

"From an *airship*?" I nearly fell out of bed. "Dad!"

Mum and Dad turned. "Oh, there you are," said Dad. "Yes, I rang the British Airship Association yesterday, but they said you'd have to go to Germany or Italy to get passenger flights. So I explained the situation and they gave me this fellow's number. He's the pilot, and he says he can take us up today, after they—"

"*Today?*"

I couldn't believe it. Was it some sort of joke? Dad was

beaming round at everyone. Ella was hopping up and down, tugging on Dad's arm.

"What's happening?" she said. "Dad? Are we still going to school? Are we going to be on the telly?"

I scrambled out of bed and into the hall. "It's even better than that," I told her. "Just you wait and see."

LIST NO.8 FANTASTIC AIRSHIP FACTS

1. The first airship was built in 1784, when Jean-Pierre Blanchard fitted a hand propeller to a balloon.

2. The first powered airship was built in 1852 by an inventor called Henri Giffard. It was powered by steam.

3. One of the most famous airships was the Hindenburg. It was like a big flying hotel, but it caught fire in 1937 and exploded.

4. In World War Two, airships escorted about 89,000 convoys of ships carrying food and supplies. None of the ships was ever sunk by enemy fire. The airships floated above enemy U-boats and bombed them. They were brilliant because they flew very slowly and couldn't be picked up on radar.

5. Airships are not very good at attacking, but they are excellent at defence.

6. A Skyship 600 (which I flew in) is 59 metres long and 20.3 metres high. It has a diameter of 15.3 metres and its envelope volume is 7,004 cubic metres.

Port Side Elevation

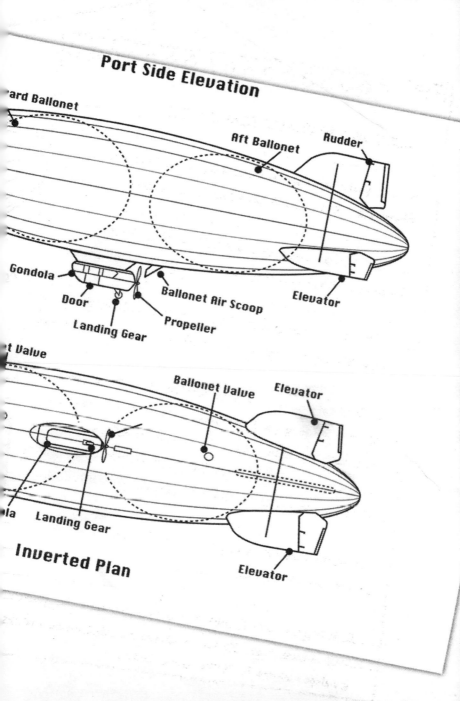

...ard Ballonet

Aft Ballonet

Rudder

Gondola

Door

Landing Gear

Propeller

Ballonet Air Scoop

Elevator

...t Valve

Ballonet Valve

Elevator

...la

Landing Gear

Elevator

Inverted Plan

PERFECT   6th March

Some things are perfect, from start to finish.

That's what going up in an airship was like.

We had to drive all day, nearly. It was very cold. There was a creamy white sky, with no clouds, and only the faint, silver disc of a sun. Most of the snow had gone and what was left clung in pale, frozen icebergs on the motorway verge. Me and Ella were buried under duvets and blankets in the back of the car.

The airship was in a big field under Helvellyn, all bustling with people and trucks and equipment. It was moored to a mobile boom truck, which is a sort of van with a boom on top of it, which can be attached to the front of the airship. There were about twenty people looking after it. We had to wait for ages while they did things like check the instruments and refuel the engines. Then Stanley and the co-pilot, Raoul, showed us the inside.

Most of an airship is the envelope, which is like a long, bean-shaped hot air balloon. All the bits that aren't the envelope are in a cabin at the bottom called a gondola. There are engines at the back, a cabin with seats for passengers to sit, and a flight compartment, which is where the pilots sit. The flight compartment has two seats, lots of dials and meters and a wheel, which you use to steer. Stanley and Raoul let me and Ella sit in the pilot seats and they spent ages telling us what everything did. Then they made us go back to the passenger bit. We were the only passengers.

The third best thing about an airship is taking off. First you get the excitement as the engines begin to whirr. The noise gets louder and louder until suddenly the airship shoots almost straight up, so you're pushed right back into your seat. It's brilliant.

When the airship had levelled off, we were allowed to take off our seatbelts and move around. Stanley and Raoul let us go in the flight compartment while they were flying. Stanley let me hold the wheel and turn it right and left. So I have flown an airship! That was the second best thing.

Stanley told us all about how you become an airship pilot. He said he started out flying aeroplanes, but then he tried airships and he liked them better. You can look out of the windows at the ground in an airship and you can see all the birds flying past, rather than just zooming by them like planes do.

"Sometimes," he said, "flocks of ducks overtake us, look back and laugh!"

The absolute best thing about the airship was what you saw out of the windows, though. You were allowed to open them and lean right out, so you got the wind blowing all in your face and in your hair. You could see everything really clearly, like a picture, all the tiny hills and mountains and lakes, drifting slowly past below you.

It felt very funny, looking out, because you were sort of separate from everything – you couldn't talk to anyone down there or swim in the lakes or climb the hills – but at the same time you were still kind of part of it. It was as though you were looking at a picture, except you weren't outside the frame. You were still there. You were just looking at it all from a different angle, from very far away.

LIST NO. 9 BEST THINGS

1. Playing long games of Warhammer with Felix. The kind where we end up having big fights with pieces and forgetting about who's winning.

2. Flying an airship.

3. The big water fight we had at school camp where everything got soaked - including all the food for the week.

4. Blowing things up with Mrs. Willis.

5. The time in hospital when we stole a trolley and spent all afternoon sliding down corridors in it while everyone on the ward was looking for us.

6. Sledging.

7. When I got to the top of the down-escalator.

8. Going on the Ultimate roller coaster twelve times in a row at Lightwater Valley with my cousins.

9. Coming downhill on a bike, as fast as you can, not braking until you get right to the bottom.

10. Feeling I can do anything. Even go to the moon.

A DECISION   7th March

The morning after we got home, Annie came to see us. She came twice; the first time to do a blood test and clean my line and the second time to give me platelets.

The second time, she sat on the floor and talked to me. I told her all about the airship and the cottage we slept in and I showed her the photos on Dad's camera.

"It sounds wonderful," she said.

"It was," I said. "It was amazing. The best ever."

"That's really great, Sam. But listen, tell me. How are you feeling? In yourself?"

I didn't want to talk about that. "I'm OK."

"Oh, Sam," said Mum. She looked at Annie. "I've been wanting to talk to you, actually. He's been very tired, falling asleep during the day – I thought it might be the morphine, but. . ."

"I didn't fall asleep on the airship," I said angrily. I didn't see why Mum had to tell Annie all this stuff. But I suppose Annie knew it all already. Mum carried on talking anyway.

"He's had more bone pain too, though we've got that under control now. I wondered. . ." She stopped. "The stuff they've been giving him from the hospital doesn't seem to be doing much any more. Should we talk to Bill, try something else?"

For a long moment, Annie didn't answer. Then she said, "If the chemotherapy really isn't working, there isn't a lot else we can offer at this stage."

My stomach clenched. I *knew* Annie would say that. Beside me, Mum tensed. She said, "But I thought . . . Bill said we'd get a year."

"Up to a year," said Annie. She looked at me. "I'm sorry." She did look sorry.

"But. . ." Mum sounded frightened. "Are we supposed to just *stop*?"

I didn't want to listen. I leaned against Mum and rested my head against her chest. She put her arm around me.

"No one's going to force either of you to do anything you don't want to do," Annie was saying. "But. . ."

"You, you, you," I thought. It's *me* that has to take it! I felt my face grow hot with anger. I thought about it all, all the pills and needles and hospital waiting rooms, that didn't make me better. They were such stupid things to spend my time worrying about.

"I want to stop," I said. "Annie said – it doesn't work any more. I think you should stop fussing about it."

Annie broke off. She and Mum looked at me. "Are you sure?" Annie said.

"Yes," I said. I was. "It's my life. I don't want to spend it taking stupid things that don't do anything."

My muscles tightened, waiting for Mum to fight. She didn't. She just nodded a few times and gave a shaky little laugh. "Right," she said. "Right. Well." She took a deep breath. "How . . . I mean how . . . how long do we have if he stops taking anything?"

Annie reached up and took Mum's hand. "It could be anything up to two months," she said. "Or it might only be a couple of weeks."

Mum nodded. "Two months," she said, and the tears spilled out of her eyes. "Bloody God!" she cried. "We were supposed to get a year."

I buried my head in her shoulder. "Don't cry," I said. "Please. I'll tell Him it's not good enough," I said, to make her smile. "When I see Him."

Mum squeezed my shoulder. "You do that," she said. She gave a shaky little laugh. "Tell Him we want our money back."

Later, after they'd both gone, I sat with the cat on my lap, looking out of the window. Columbus butted his head against my wrist, wanting to be stroked. I felt dull and heavy all over. "Two months," I thought. And then, "Two weeks!"

I wished Felix were here. I wondered what he'd say. I imagined him, leaning back in his chair, his old fedora hat pulled low over his forehead. "Two weeks!" I told him.

"Oh, well," the imaginary Felix said cheerfully. "Make the most of it. I would. Just think – they'll never say no to you ever again!"

I blinked. Would Felix really say that? Maybe. I thought about it. "There isn't anything else I want," I told him. It was true. Nothing Mum or Dad could give me anyway.

Felix shook his head. "I thought you were going to see the Earth from space?" he said. "You never did that, did you?"

I sat up a bit. "That wasn't a real one," I said. "Not one to really do."

But Felix never let me get away with that. We'd done a world record. We'd seen a ghost. Kind of. Even an imaginary Felix wouldn't let me get away with that.

"Wimp," he said. "Go on." He grinned at me. "I dare you."

QUESTIONS NOBODY ANSWERS NO. 8

Will the world still be there when I am gone?

THE MOON AND THE APPLE TREE 8th March

When I was a little kid I saw a TV programme with an astronaut talking about seeing the Earth from above. It's like a giant globe in space, only alive, and you can see the seas and the mountains and the cities and all the clouds moving and swirling and you're like, *the whole entire human race except for me is there.* I remember watching and thinking, "I'm going to do that when I grow up." I didn't realize then how difficult it would be.

And now it was the only thing left on my list to do.

I sat and tried to work out how somebody could do it. Maybe you could ring up a charity and ask them to fly you to America and blast you up. But probably not. Or maybe there was a cheaty way of doing it. Like, I've seen the Earth from an airship. Did that count? And I've seen photographs from space. That's *sort of* doing it. Except it wasn't what I'd wanted. It was like saying you wanted to meet the Queen and getting a photograph instead.

I stayed on the sofa for a long time, not doing anything, just thinking about it. Then I fell asleep.

When I woke up, I was in my own bed. It was the middle of the night. My room was very dark. Too dark. The shadows looked wrong, like when it snowed and the light was suddenly brighter – like that, only this time everything was darker. I lay on my side, trying to understand the new strangeness. Then I realized. The streetlight outside my window was gone.

I sat up and pressed the light switch. Nothing happened. "A power cut!" I thought. "It's night-time and there's been a power cut and everyone except me is asleep." As I thought it, I was filled with a strange, quivery excitement. All of a sudden, I couldn't stay in bed.

I got up and went into the kitchen. I know where we keep the torch – in the muddle drawer, with the hammers and wire and glue – but I had to scrabble for ages before I found it. I was terrified that Mum or Dad would hear me and come down. When I went into the hall to look for my coat, I didn't dare turn on the torch in case they saw it. In the end I put on Dad's jacket and Granny's walking hat and Mum's trainers and went outside like that.

It wasn't as cold as I'd thought it would be. It was eerily bright. Our garden wasn't a garden; it was a mass of bright, silvery shadows and dark lumps that turned into trees and bushes when I shone the torch on them. And it was very, very still. I stood for a long time on the doorstep, picking things out. *There's* the patio, where I used to spread out all my Lego. *That's* the pond that my cousin Pete and I made. We spent all day digging at it. And then my dad and Uncle Leigh finished it off properly and Pete and I stole some frogspawn from Granny's allotment to put in. There are still frogs in there now. The great-grandfrogs of our tadpoles.

The pond looked bigger in the dark. It's not actually that wide. Me and Ella can jump over it, no problem. Or we *could*. I hadn't tried since I got ill again. "I dare you," I thought, "I dare you," and then I knew I had to do it.

I looked at the pond, making sure of how far I'd have to jump, trying not to think about what would happen if I missed. Then I ran up to the edge, and leaped.

I landed heavily and fell forward on to my hands and knees, breathless, the torch falling on to the grass and rolling forward. I froze, expecting to hear Mum or Dad calling. They didn't. I sat up and inspected myself. No blood. Bruises, probably, but I've got lots of bruises already anyway, so it doesn't matter. "I did it!" I thought. This thrill of excitement ran through me and I thought, "What shall I do next?"

Our garden isn't that big. There's the pond and the lawn, with splodge-shaped flowerbeds growing in the middle of it, all very neat. At the bottom there's the apple tree and a hedge with a fence behind it. You can squeeze all the way along between the hedge and the fence, like a secret passage.

"That's what I'll do," I thought. "I'll go through the secret passage in the middle of the night." But when I got there and saw the apple tree, I had a better idea. I put my torch in my jacket pocket and started to climb.

It was harder than I'd thought. For one thing, I was wearing Mum's trainers and they kept trying to fall off. I had to keep my toes clenched tightly inside them. And I was only wearing pyjamas, so my legs kept getting scraped. I used to climb up the apple tree every autumn, no problem. But this time was the hardest it'd ever been. It was hard finding all the footholds. Even pulling myself on to the next branch was harder. It stopped being fun. "I'm going to fall out," I thought. "I'm going to fall out, I'm going to fall out." I knew I ought to go back. But I didn't. I kept right on pulling myself up, even though my arms and legs were aching, until I got to the top.

And that's when I saw it.

We don't get stars properly where I live. We get some, but not really. Dad says it's the streetlights. But that night they were all off. All you could see, for miles and miles and miles, right up until the universe curled around the edges of the sky, were stars. There was Orion and the Plough and lots of others I didn't know the name of. And there, huge and round and sort of silvery-shiny, was the Moon.

I stared and stared. I'd never seen the Moon that big or that bright. It looked like someone had cut it out of silver paper with big school scissors and stuck it on to the sky. I don't know why it was so good – maybe because I was still tired and tingly or maybe just because I was absolutely alone in absolute middle-of-the-night-ness, or maybe because of what Annie had told me. I don't know. I sat there for what felt like hours and stared and stared and stared.

I don't want to write about climbing down or trying to find pyjamas without green branchy mess on them, when all I wanted was to sleep for hours and hours. The Moon and the sky were the important bits. And I know what I did wasn't the same as seeing the Earth from space – it wasn't what I'd wanted, when I wrote it – but that's OK. It was the *feeling* I wanted and I got that.

Isn't it funny? When I wrote that list, I never, ever thought I'd do half those things. They weren't things to do. They were just . . . things. Ideas.

And now I've done them all.

WHY DO WE HAVE TO DIE ANYWAY?

I can understand dying when it's old people. You wouldn't want to live forever. I read a book once where some people did and they didn't like it much. They just got bored and old and lonely and sad. And then there's practical things too. Like, if no one died and people kept getting born, the world would get fuller and fuller, until everyone would be standing on everyone else's heads, and we'd all have to live underwater, or on Mars, and even then there wouldn't be enough room, probably.

I know all that.

But it doesn't explain why kids have to die.

Granny says looking at it like that is all wrong. She says dying is like caterpillars turning into butterflies. She says, of course it's scary, just as it's scary for caterpillars going into cocoons. But what would happen, she says, if caterpillars went around going, "Oh no, I'm about to go into a cocoon, it's so unfair"? They'd never turn into butterflies, that's what.

What she means is, it's the next stage in a life cycle. Like turning into Spiderman was the next stage in Peter Parker's life cycle. So you shouldn't be frightened, you should be excited. But I'm not frightened anyway. It's only going back to wherever you were before you were born and no one is frightened of before they were born.

We used to do life cycles at my old school. I know the water cycle and the carbon cycle and the how-new-stars-get-born cycle. They're all about old things dying and new things getting born. Old stars turning into new ones. Dead leaves turning into baby plants. It might be something dying or it might be something getting born. It all depends how you look at it.

DIFFERENT

Things are different now.

I don't go to clinic any more. Annie comes more often. If she doesn't come, she rings Mum up and talks to her.

People keep coming to see us. Grandma and Grandpa came all the way from Orkney and stayed with Granny. Auntie Jane came and gave me a wooden elephant and Auntie Nicola came down from Edinburgh, gave me a book about castles, and went back up the same night. Uncle Richard came while I was working with Mrs Willis, deciding what order to put all the lists and stories and things in my book. Mum said I had to come and talk to him and I wouldn't. Mum got angry and said he'd come all the way from

Lincoln to see me. I got angry too. I don't want to be nice to aunts and uncles all day.

"I want to do my things!" I said. "I don't have any time to do my things!" I bent my head over my piece of paper and wouldn't look at her.

Mrs Willis said maybe she shouldn't come as often.

"No!" I said. "I want you to keep coming."

Uncle Richard got very flustered and said he didn't want to cause any trouble. He gave me a jumper that said "SURFING USA" on it and then he and Mum sat on the sofa talking while me and Mrs Willis tried to work.

After that, Mum said people could only stay for twenty minutes and not when I was doing school. School isn't as regular as it used to be, anyway. Mrs Willis rings up before she comes, in case I'm asleep or something. I sleep quite a lot. It comes in useful. Mum's friend Maureen came round three times to see me last week and I just squeezed my eyes tight shut and pretended to be asleep.

Ella is funny too. People keep wanting to take her out to the cinema or to dancing lessons or something, but she never will. She won't go to school either. Mum has a big fight with her every morning. Mostly Mum makes her go, but sometimes she gets to stay at home. When she's allowed to stay, she does her Good Brownie routine. She comes up to me and puts her hands behind her back and says, "Mum says do you want anything?"

That's Mum's way of saying, "Do you want something to eat?"

She had a big talk with Annie about me not eating properly. Now she doesn't make me eat dinners, but she keeps feeding me bits of things like fruit or ice cream. So yesterday I said, "Yes, I want a bottle of beer and a speedboat." Ella started giggling and ran back to Mum. She was gone for ages. Then she came back in a big apron, like a chef, with a tray and a bottle of beer that she'd got from next door, giggling away.

Yesterday, Mum let her stay at home because I had a big nosebleed in the middle of the night and woke everyone up. Mrs Willis said she could do lessons with us.

"You don't want to write a book too, do you?" she said. Ella shook her head.

"I'm going to do pictures for Sam's book," she said.

I don't want Ella's babyish pictures in my book, but I didn't say so. Maybe she can have *one*. She drew a picture yesterday of us all. Mum and Dad were holding hands and me and Ella were waving. There was black spiky grass, and flowers, and a great big sun with great big sun rays wobbling all over the sky.

This is Ella's picture.

CLAY BIRDS   29th March

I don't just sleep a lot. When I'm not asleep, I can't wake up properly. I'm tired and I ache all over. I can't write and I can't think.

When Mrs Willis came today, I said I didn't want to work. She didn't make me. Instead, she brought a bucket of clay from her car and we made things. We put newspapers over the coffee table in the living room and spread the clay all over them. Some fell off and got on the carpet, but Mum didn't fuss. She said it would all come out with soap and water, all come out in the wash, she said, and it did.

The clay was perfect, wet-dark and slippery-smooth. I held it and squeezed it and it oozed out from the bottom of one hand

and into the palm of the other. I made it into balls and little aeroplanes and fake fossils to bury in the garden and confuse geologists. I wrote my name in it with the knife. Sam Oliver McQueen. S.O.M. Sam.

Mrs Willis made me a little ship, with a mast and a clay sail but no keel, because it's a sailing ship and you can't see the keel under the water. It has a flag at the top of the mast, clay bent to look as if it's flying.

"Where's it going?" she said,

and I said, "Africa."

I made a round clay bird for Ella, a blackbird because she has black hair. I made an owl for Dad with round owl glasses like he has and feathers drawn on with a knife. I made Mum a sparrow because of the Bible story about the sparrows who were sold for two-a-penny. Nobody thought they were worth anything, but God knew all of them by name.

Mrs Willis said she would take my birds and my boat and bake them in her friend's kiln and then they would harden and set forever. She said next time she came, we could paint them properly and I could give them as presents.

I could give them as soon as the paint was dry, she said. Or I could save them and give them later, if I wanted.

POST CARD

Dear Sam,
Thank you so much for letting
us show you our ship. Hope
you enjoyed the day as much
as we did!
Here's a DVD of our advert,
which will be broadcast in
the autumn.
    All the best,
        Stanley & Raoul

Dear Sam,
    I am sending you two
Spiderman videos, a book of
football stickers and a telescope.
Also some of my brother's
more awful music. Enjoy.
        Yours,
        Mickey
    PS Love from Mum.

98109750091

Dear Sam,
Thinking of you.
With much love.
Grandma and
Grandpa
xxx

thinking of you

GEORGIA O'KEEFFE (1887–1986)
Barn with Snow, 1933
Oil on Canvas

Dear Sam,
We all miss you at dinner—
bet you don't miss us!
Here's a true fact for your
book: more people donate
blood if you DON'T pay
them than if you do.
Explain that if you can.
From Dr Bill

PRESENTS   3rd April

Today, Mrs Willis brought my birds back.

The fire of the kiln had hardened the clay and turned it a pale pink. We looked up sparrows and owls and blackbirds in Mum's big bird book, to get the colours just right. I made Dad an eagle owl, because they're so big and fierce-looking. They have sticky-up ear tufts, but I just painted those on the top of my owl's head. Mum's bird was a hedge sparrow, with a grey belly and little eyes. Hedge sparrows and eagle owls look different but they're the same colours: brown, with black spots.

"Birds of a feather flock together," said Mrs Willis and she put them side by side to dry.

Ella's bird was easy. Shiny black feathers and a yellow beak, although really girl blackbirds aren't black. The blackbird in the book had his head in the air and a glint in his eye. It looked a bit like Ella, squaring up for a fight.

"Ella's going to be all right," I thought, and I painted a smile on her bird. Birds don't smile, really, but then owls don't wear glasses either and Dad's was, so it didn't matter.

After Mrs Willis had gone, I fell asleep again. When I woke up, I lay on the sofa and thought about her and Granny and Annie. They ought to have presents too, but I didn't have any more clay and I didn't know how to make anything else, except cakes. And you can't keep cakes. I wanted a present that meant they wouldn't forget me. I mean, I know Granny's got lots of photographs of me, but Annie and Mrs Willis haven't.

I got up and went to find Mum. She was sitting at the table looking out at the garden.

"Hello, sweetheart," she said when I came and sat down by her. She put her arm round me. "How are you feeling?"

"Fine," I said. I rested my head against her. "Do you have any photos of me?"

"I think I might have one or two somewhere," said Mum. "Why?"

"I want to make something for Annie and Granny and Mrs Willis. I thought I could do photo frames, with pictures, only we've used up all the clay."

"I'm sure we can think of something," said Mum.

We had a good afternoon. Mum found me some old picture frames and we stuck them all over with the little tiles left over from the bathroom. When the glue was dry, we covered all the spaces with grout, so you couldn't see any of the old frames. Anyone who came to visit, we made help. I fell asleep while they were finishing them. When I woke up, Mum and Mum's vicar and two old ladies from her church were all sitting there with grouty hands, making picture frames.

This is the Earth from space. I am here.

Saturday 04

4

This is the view from our airship.

THE AVENGING ANGEL

This is a beer mat from the Avenging Angel

When I woke up today, the sun was shining through the windows. I lay on my side and watched the sunlight dancing on the wall. The air was bright and full of light.

I got up and went into the living room. I walked very slowly and carefully. I felt strange and light-headed. The world looked different, kind of the way it does, sometimes, when you realize that you're a person looking at the world and you suddenly think how weird that is. That's a sofa, that's Ella's old elephant, that's an IV stand – it's like you're looking at them on a TV screen for the first time and you realize how strange it is that you're in the world, looking at these very bright and *here* things and how you're *here* too, but at the same time you're kind of not, you're separate, watching it all from somewhere else.

Maybe you don't know what I mean. But that's how I felt.

Ella was sitting on the sofa, watching cartoons in her pyjamas. Mum and Dad and Granny were sharing the big Saturday newspaper on the dining table. They looked up as I came through.

"Look," said Mum, holding out her hand. "Spring's come."

I looked out of the window. The sun was shining, the sky was blue from edge to edge and you could see for the first time where new little leaves were uncurling on the trees.

I sat down by Dad. I still felt strange. Sort of not quite connected to the rest of the world.

"Annie's coming round in a bit," said Mum.

"Can we invite Mrs Willis too?" I said. I looked at her meaningfully. She got it straight away.

"Of course. We could all go and sit out in the garden."

It was a bit cold to sit in the garden, but nobody cared. Mum fussed around for ages making tea and offering people biscuits and I kept going, "Mum. *Mu-um*," until *finally* she put down the teapot and said, "Sam has something for you."

They liked their presents. Dad liked the eagle owl so much, he said he was going to buy some hair gel and make himself ear tufts to scare all the people who work for him. Mrs Willis said she'd never had a nicer present and it was even better than a kid she'd once taught who'd given her one of his kidney stones. All the grown-ups sat and talked for ages and ages. Ella got bored and went off to play swing-tennis, but I didn't feel like it. I sat watching them all, trying to hold them tight and safe in my memory, until I fell asleep.

LIST NO. 10 WHERE DO YOU GO AFTER YOU DIE?

1. You might become a ghost and haunt people. You could visit your family and let them know you're OK. You could fly, and stay up all night, and get into theme parks and cinemas for free.

2. You might be reincarnated and get born again as someone - or something - else. I want to be a wolf. Or an alien.

3. You might go to Heaven.

4. You might go to Hell.

5. You might go to Purgatory, which is where you get sent if you aren't good enough for Heaven or bad enough for Hell. You float around in Purgatory for years and years and years until you're good enough to get into Heaven.

6. You might sort of become part of everything and drift around being a cloud or a tree.

7. It might just be like falling asleep.

8. It might be a mixture of these. Or some people might do one thing and some poeple might do another.

9. It might be something else entirely. Nobody knows.

DREAMING

This time when I fell asleep, I dreamed.

I dreamed I was sleeping in Mum and Dad's big bed again. Mum and Dad were there too, and Ella. It was very early in the morning. I could see the light coming through the windows and the sky, pale and fragile and still. There were no clouds. I could see everything very sharp and clear. I could see the curtains moving in the breeze from the window. I could see the apple tree in the garden, all covered in new little leaves.

In my dream, we were all asleep. Ella was sleeping on her back, next to me. Her face was pink and I could see the muscles moving under her skin, so I knew she was dreaming. Dad had his arm around her. The back of his hand was just brushing against mine. Mum was sleeping on her side. She was curved around me. I could feel her hair against my neck, soft and light.

I was sleeping too, warm there in the middle of my family-nest, but it was as if I was outside myself. I was watching myself sleeping, from above. There were no bright lights. There were no angels. There was just Mum and Dad and Ella, all asleep on the big bed with me there above them, watching as they got smaller and smaller and further and further away.

I woke. I was lying in the big bed, just like in my dream. The room was full of pale light and soft with early morning quiet. Mum was asleep on her side. Dad was lying awake beside me. When he saw me watching, he smiled.

"Hey," he said, and stretched out his hand. I held it loosely in mine.

"Why am I in your bed?" I said.

"Because you've got a temperature," he said.

I lay there, quiet. I felt very strange. It was as if my body didn't belong to me any more; as if I were floating just above it. It felt heavy and old and very, very tired.

"I love you," said Dad suddenly.

He seemed very far away and unimportant.

"I know," I said.

We lay there, just the two of us, very quiet and still, me holding his fingers between mine. Then I closed my eyes again and drifted back into sleep.

1. Sam died on 14th April at about 5.30 am

2. The cause of death was

   Acute lymphoblastic Leukaemia

3. Sam's death was:
   (a.) Peaceful.
   b. Horrible and agonizingly painful.
   c. Kind of in the middle.
   d. We don't know, we were at the chip shop.
   e. Other, please specify.

4. He was:
   (a.) At home.
   b. In hospital.
   c. At his best friend Felix's house.
   d. On the number 37 bus.
   e. Other, please specify.

5. The people with him were:
   (a.) All his family. Mum, Dad and Ella.
   b. Nobody.
   c. Random medical people.

    d. The Queen.
    e. Other, please specify.

6. The weather was:
    a. Warm.
    b. Cold.
    (c.) In-between.
    d. Raining fish.
    e. Other, please specify.

7. Other information:

Sam died quietly in his sleep.
He was in no pain

LIST NO. 11 THINGS I WANT TO HAPPEN AFTER
I AM DEAD

1. I think a funeral should be fun. People shouldn't wear black. You should tell funny stories about me, not sad ones.

2. Anyone who wants to read my book can. It's not a secret.

3. You should give most of my things away. You can keep some of them, but you don't have to keep them all.

4. Ella should have my bedroom, because it is bigger than hers.

5. She can have my bike and my Playstation too.

6. You're allowed to be sad, but you aren't allowed to be too sad. If you're always sad when you think about me, then how can you remember me?

ACKNOWLEDGEMENTS

First of all, huge thanks to Julia Green and everyone on the wonderful MA in Writing for Young People at Bath Spa: Sandra-Lynne Jones, Kellie Jones, Julia Draper, Sian Price, Tara Button, Sarah Oliver, Lucy Staff, Sarah Lee and Liz Kernoghan. Without you this book would never have been written. Thank you for your encouragement, for saying, "No, Sally," week after week and for all your invaluable suggestions.

Thank you to CLIC nurses at the Royal United Hospital in Bath and to the Children's Hospice in Bristol for answering all my questions. Particular thanks to Cylla Cole at the Bristol Royal Hospital for Children for her enthusiasm and for reading the manuscript before publication. Thanks to Anna James for telling me about platelets ("yellow and squishy") and children's oncology wards ("surprisingly cheerful") and for letting me see her Hickman Line.

Thank you to my dear mum for believing in me and supporting me and to my family for all the bits of real life I borrowed for the book. Thank you to the Republic of Stanley Road for saying, "Of course you should be a writer!" and laughing at me in such an encouraging way. Thank you to Tom Harris for smiling at me lovingly over the top of a laptop. Thank you to Raoul Sullivan for telling me about how great airships are. Thank you to Rosemary Canter for saying yes.

Finally, thank you to Oliviero Muzi-Falconi for being the handwriting of Sam. Thanks to Filippo Muzi-Falconi for drawing Sam's pictures, to Freya Wilson for drawing Ella's, and to Nikalas Catlow for Dad's. Also thanks to Caro Humphries and Tom Harris, for providing handwriting.

Sally Nicholls
London, 2007

WEBSITES

www.clicsargent.org.uk
CLIC Sargent

www.leukaemia.org
Children with Leukaemia

www.macmillan.org.uk
Macmillan Cancer Support

www.helpthehospices.org.uk
National hospice charity

FICTION FOR YOUNG PEOPLE

Two Weeks with the Queen by Morris Gleitzman

Charlotte's Web by E. B. White

Becky Bananas: This Is Your Life! by Jean Ure

Through a Glass, Darkly by Jostein Gaarder

FICTION FOR ADULTS

Oscar and the Lady in Pink by Eric-Emmanuel Schmitt

Spoonface Steinberg a play by Lee Hall

REFERENCE BOOKS

The Private Worlds of Dying Children by Myra Bluebond-Langner

On Death and Dying by Elisabeth Kübler-Ross

Living with Death and Dying by Elisabeth Kübler-Ross

Final Gifts: Understanding and Helping the Dying by Maggie Callanan and Patricia Kelley

Sally Nicholls

was born in Stockton, just after midnight, in a thunderstorm. Her father died when she was two, and she and her brother were brought up by her mother. She has always loved reading, and spent most of her childhood trying to make real life work like it did in books. After school, she worked in Japan for six months and travelled around Australia and New Zealand, then came back and did a degree in Philosophy and Literature at Warwick. In her third year she enrolled in a Masters in Writing for Young People at Bath Spa University. It was here, at the age of twenty-two, that she wrote Ways to Live Forever, her first novel. Sally is now living in London where she works part-time and continues to write.

www.sallynicholls.com

To find out more about Sally Nicholls,
or just to tell us what you think about
this extraordinary novel please visit:

www.waystoliveforever.co.uk